STILL A NATION OF IMMIGRANTS

Taking the Oath of Allegiance at citizenship ceremonies, Bryant Center, Alexandria, Virginia.

STILL A NATION OF IMMIGRANTS

Brent Ashabranner

Photographs by Jennifer Ashabranner

COBBLEHILL BOOKS/Dutton

New York

Quotation on page 119 is used by permission of the University Press of New England. Credit: Lawrence H. Fuchs, *The American Kaleidoscope*, pg. 5, copyright 1990 by Lawrence H. Fuchs, Wesleyan University Press.

Library of Congress Cataloging-in-Publication Data
Ashabranner, Brent K., date.
Still a nation of immigrants / Brent Ashabranner ; photographs by Jennifer Ashabranner.
p.   cm.
Includes bibliographical references and index.
Summary: Identifies who today's immigrants to the United States are, describes their experiences, contributions, and impact on society, and discusses how an immigrant becomes a citizen.
ISBN 0-525-65130-6
1. United States—Emigration and immigration—Juvenile literature.   2. Immigrants—United States—Juvenile literature.   [1. United States—Emigration and immigration.   2. Immigrants.]
I. Ashabranner, Jennifer, ill.   II. Title.
JV6455.A892 1993   325.73—dc20   92-44335   CIP   AC

Published in the United States by Cobblehill Books,
an affiliate of Dutton Children's Books,
a division of Penguin Books USA Inc.,
375 Hudson Street, New York, New York 10014
Designed by Joy Taylor
Printed in the United States of America
First Edition   10 9 8 7 6 5 4 3 2 1

This book is for Patt Behler

BOOKS ABOUT IMMIGRANTS AND IMMIGRATION
BY BRENT ASHABRANNER

The New Americans: Changing Patterns in U.S. Immigration
Children of the Maya: A Guatemalan Indian Odyssey
Into a Strange Land: Unaccompanied Refugee Youth in America
The Vanishing Border: A Photographic Journey Along Our
    Frontier with Mexico
An Ancient Heritage: The Arab-American Minority

Contents

Unless otherwise attributed, all immigrant statistics in this book, past and present, come from studies based on U.S. Census Bureau figures. The same is true for numbers about the general U.S. population and about racial and ethnic groups.

My demographic research was greatly facilitated by publications of the Population Reference Bureau in Washington, D.C. Most useful was the Population Bulletin "Immigration to the U.S.: The Unfinished Story" by Leon F. Bouvier and Robert W. Gardner. As always, my daughter Melissa Ashabranner gave me invaluable research assistance.

In a few places in *Still a Nation of Immigrants* I have adapted material which seemed especially pertinent from my earlier books about immigrants, particularly *The New Americans*.

Brent Ashabranner

1

Immigration to America: The Making of a Nation

---

immigrant: a person who comes to a country to take up permanent residence.

Webster's Ninth New Collegiate Dictionary

Pledging allegiance to the flag at a citizenship ceremony.

NOTHING about the Bryant Center in the Washington, D.C., suburb of Alexandria, Virginia, is memorable. Its main feature is a large auditorium with a stage at one end. The floor is gray linoleum tile; the rows of seats are rust-colored plastic; no pictures decorate the walls. It might be a civic center anywhere in the United States; yet for more than five thousand immigrants in the Washington area who take the oath of citizenship here every year, the Bryant Center will remain in their memories for a lifetime.

Jennifer and I visited the Bryant Center on a day in early spring when 259 immigrants from fifty-nine countries were to become citizens. The program preceding the oath taking was scheduled to begin at ten o'clock, but the citizens-to-be began arriving by nine, in some cases whole families. The growing crowd was quiet, subdued by the importance of the occasion. Most of the men were dressed in business suits, the women in dresses. Only a few, mostly Muslim women, wore the national dress of their homeland.

3

Promptly at ten o'clock an honor guard from the local American Legion post presented the American flag. A voice over the loudspeaker said, "It is customary for everyone to stand when the colors are presented."

Everyone stood. A trio of young women from the Environmental Protection Agency sang "The Star-Spangled Banner." Then William Carroll, district director of the U.S. Immigration and Naturalization Service, took his place behind the podium onstage. Mr. Carroll probably has presided over more citizenship ceremonies than any other official in the country, but nothing about his welcoming remarks was routine or casual. He seemed to be speaking directly to each person when he said, "Today marks a new start for you, a rebirth in a new land. Citizenship gives you the same privileges as those born here and requires the same responsibilities."

Then Carroll talked about his grandfather who was an immigrant from Italy. "I remember that I once asked my grandfather, 'Why did you come to America?' And my grandfather told me, 'I could have gone anywhere. I could have gone to France, but I could never have been a Frenchman. I could have gone to England, but I could never have been an Englishman. But when I came to America, I could become an American.' This process of new people entering this country and becoming Americans continues to this day and will continue to enrich our nation in many ways."

Speeches, more singing, and a patriotic poem followed. The prospective citizens sat patiently, as did their friends and family members who had come for the ceremony. But at last the moment they had all been waiting for arrived. William Carroll returned to the podium, "Now it is time for you to take the Oath of Allegiance. Stand as the name of your *former* country is called."

A murmur ran through the oath takers when Carroll said "your *former* country," and then the auditorium became very quiet. The roll call of countries began, and people stood as the names of their countries came over the loudspeaker: Afghanistan, Argentina, Barbados, Bolivia, Canada, Chile, China, Columbia. The names continued: Equador, Egypt—Ghana, Greece—Kenya, Korea—Pakistan, Panama—until the last name, Vietnam, was called, and everyone was standing.

Then Carroll asked those becoming citizens to raise their right hands and to repeat the Oath of Allegiance after him. He read slowly and clearly, pausing often for the response:

> *I hereby declare, on oath, that I absolutely and entirely re-*
> *nounce and abjure all allegiance and fidelity to any foreign*
> *prince, potentate, state or sovereignty, of whom or which I*
> *have heretofore been a subject or citizen;*
> *that I will support and defend the Constitution and laws of*
> *the United States of America against all enemies, foreign or*
> *domestic;*
> *that I will bear true faith and allegiance to the same;*
> *that I will bear arms on behalf of the United States when re-*
> *quired by the law;*
> *that I will perform noncombatant service in the armed forces*
> *of the United States when required by the law;*
> *that I will perform work of national importance under civil-*
> *ian direction when required by the law;*
> *and that I take this obligation freely without any mental res-*
> *ervation or purpose of evasion;*
> *so help me God.*

The Oath of Allegiance has been a part of the citizenship process for a long time and today may seem a little old-fashioned, especially the reference to "fidelity to any foreign prince and potentate;" and the use of such words as "abjure" and "heretofore" may test the range of many immigrants' vocabulary. Still, the message of the oath surely comes through to almost all who take it: this is your country now, and you must do your part to keep it safe and healthy.

New citizens eager to exercise their right to vote.

The new citizens then, with hands over their hearts, said the Pledge of Allegiance to the Flag, and the ceremony was over. They filed up to the front to receive their certificates of citizenship. A woman from the Daughters of the American Revolution handed out copies of the Declaration of Independence and small American flags.

Now that the tension of the ceremony and oath taking was over, the auditorium was filled with happy, excited voices and laughter. People shook hands, embraced each other, and smiled as friends and relatives took pictures. Many of the new citizens, now eligible to vote in local and national elections, headed for voter registration tables that had been set up in the Bryant Center.

Everyone I spoke to was happy to talk. A middle-aged German said that the decision to become an American citizen had been a very difficult one for him. "When you are born German," he said, "you are a German. But America has been good to me. I have been here twenty-six years. My children are Americans. Finally I knew that I am an American, too, and that I had to become a citizen."

I talked to a young man while he waited in the voter registration line; his former country had been Guatemala. "I came here because I was caught in the political violence in my country," he said. "I thought I would return to Guatemala someday. But I had not been here long before I knew I did not want to return, and I decided to become a citizen of the United States as quickly as I could. Now I am a citizen. I will vote for president in November."

I shouldn't have asked the question, but I did. "For whom will you vote?"

The new American smiled. "In Guatemala," he said, "I would be afraid to tell you how I intend to vote. Here I am not afraid." His smile grew broader. "But I do not know yet."

A Nation of Immigrants

IN MANY cities across the United States, citizenship oath-taking ceremonies like the one in the Bryant Center are held monthly. Over a quarter of a million immigrants are now becoming American citizens every year, 270,000 in 1990, for example, about the same number in 1991. These immigrants have come from more than one hundred countries in every part of the globe; they have lived in the United States for at least five years and have met the other requirements for citizenship. Officials of the Immigration and Naturalization Service say that the number of immigrants becoming citizens annually would be even greater if the INS had enough staff to process more applications.

Almost everyone is familiar with the statement that the United States is a nation of immigrants, but what does the phrase "a nation of immigrants" really mean? It means, in the simplest terms, that if you or your parents are not yourselves immigrants, you have immigrants to

America somewhere in your family history. "All of our people all over the country," President Franklin Roosevelt once said, "except the pure-blooded Indians, are immigrants or the descendants of immigrants, including even those who came over here on the *Mayflower.*"

In fact, pure-blooded Indians are also descendants of immigrants. Their remote ancestors migrated from northeast Asia to Alaska at least thirty thousand years ago and spread throughout the Americas. Today's Indians are called Native Americans because their forebears were already here when modern immigration to America began after the voyages of Columbus made this part of the world known to Europe.

But, you may ask, what is so special about America? Isn't it true that all countries have immigrants? Haven't countries in Africa, Asia, Europe, and South America sometimes had large migrations from other countries because of war, famine, or economic conditions?

The answer to both questions is yes. But no other country in history has ever received so many people from so many parts of the world as have come to the United States. More than that, a high level of immigration has been an almost unbroken part of American life, starting in the colonial period before we became a nation and continuing to this very day.

The number and variety of people who have come from other lands to this land, and who continue to come, make the United States uniquely a nation of immigrants.

All immigrant groups have brought with them their particular cultures: language, religion, ideas, customs, music, food—everything that makes a culture. Drawing richly from these many different cultures, a new culture, an American culture, has been forged over the centuries. It is in this most fundamental sense that we are a nation of immigrants.

European immigrants are crammed aboard this ship bringing them to the United States about the turn of this century.

The Roots of Nationhood

THE ORIGINAL thirteen colonies from which our nation grew were settled by immigrants from England and a few other European countries. After the colonial period, immigration from Great Britain continued to dominate, although German immigrants began to come in increasing numbers to the new nation which called itself the United States of America. An estimated quarter of a million immigrants arrived from Europe between the end of the Revolutionary War and 1819, and English was firmly established as the language of the United States.

The importation of slaves to the United States was outlawed in 1808. But before this law's passage, over half a million Africans had been brought to North America in forced immigration, and the new law had no effect on enslaved persons already in the country. In human terms, the early roots of America were in both European and African soil.

The year 1819 marked the beginning of reasonably good record keeping on immigrants to the United States. A federal law passed that year required the captain of every ship docking at a U.S. port to give customs officials a list of all passengers on board. Immigrants arriving overland from Canada or Mexico often were not counted, but they were relatively few compared to arrivals by ship. The early records show that between 1820 and 1890 at least 83 percent of all immigrants came from England, Scotland, Ireland, Germany, and other northern and western European countries.

During the decade 1880–1889 immigration to America began a sharp increase. In that ten-year period more than 5 million new arrivals were recorded, double the number of any previous census decade. In 1885 the Statue of Liberty, a gift from France, was assembled on Bedloe's Island—now named Liberty Island—in New York Harbor. As if the majestic new statue, her torch of liberty held high, beckoned the poor and oppressed from across the ocean, immigration continued its dramatic surge, reaching its highest level between 1900 and 1909 when 8.8 million immigrants arrived on U.S. soil. In the half century 1880–1929, over 27 million people came to America to live.

Behind the remarkable growth of America's immigrant population in the late nineteenth and early twentieth centuries lay dramatic changes in America itself. Primarily an agricultural country before the Civil War, the United States became an industrial giant with astonishing speed in the postwar era. Coal mines, oil fields and refineries, steel mills, textile mills and factories, automotive plants, and an expanding railroad system were but a part of this industrial explosion.

The new industries needed people, in many cases people willing to work for low wages in jobs that more often than not were hard, dangerous, and monotonous. The federal government printed leaflets advertising opportunities in America and distributed them in several European countries. Some states, notably Pennsylvania and Illinois, sent recruiting agents to Europe to attract immigrants. Private companies established recruiting programs in Europe. If recruiters painted a falsely rosy picture of life in America, they were only saying the things that the landless, poverty-stricken masses of Europe longed to hear.

For fifty years the Statue of Liberty was the first sight that millions of immigrants had of what was to be their new homeland. Even if they could not read Emma Lazarus's poem cast in bronze on the statue, they must have felt its meaning as they sailed close to the great lady holding high her torch of liberty. The poem concludes:

> *Give me your tired, your poor,*
> *Your huddled masses yearning to breathe free,*
> *The wretched refuse of your teeming shore.*
> *I lift my lamp beside the golden door.*

Once inside the "golden door" of New York Harbor, the immigrants' first stop was the mammoth new receiving center on Ellis Island. Immigration procedures were in an early stage of development, and Ellis Island must have been a Tower of Babel as officials with little training and experience listened to dozens of languages and dialects and tried to record information about the new arrivals. The medical examinations given were rudimentary at best, but about 2 percent of all those who reached Ellis Island were turned back for either physical or mental medical problems.

Ellis Island was closed in 1954 and had not been used as an immigrant receiving facility for years before that. But during its heyday,

Immigrants await entry to the United States at Ellis Island.

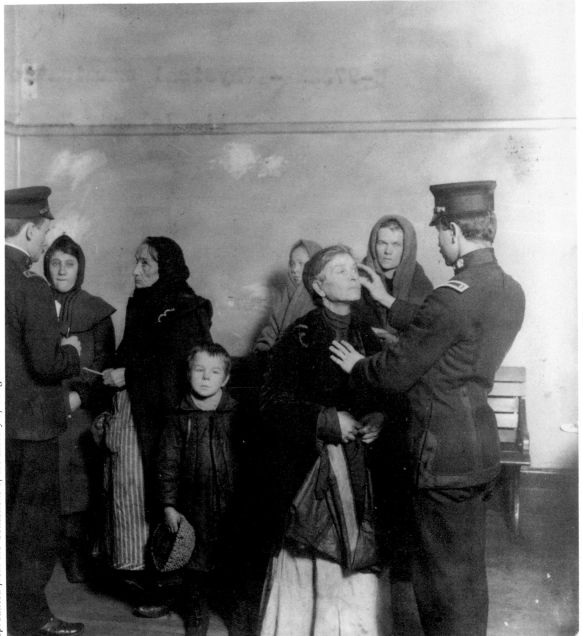

Health examinations at Ellis Island were usually hasty and superficial.

between 1892 and 1924, 12 million immigrants were processed there, and today 100 million Americans, 40 percent of our current population, trace their ancestry to someone who passed through Ellis Island. Abandoned and left in a state of decay for three decades, the Main Building of Ellis Island has now been restored, filled with fascinating exhibits, and is open to the public as the Ellis Island Immigration Museum.

IN THE last decade of the nineteenth century, a great influx of immigrants from southern and eastern Europe, notably Italy and Russia, ended western and northern Europe's long domination of immigration to America. By 1910 immigrants from the south and east of Europe equaled those coming from Great Britain and such other countries as Germany and Sweden. In the decade 1910–1919 immigration from southern and eastern Europe exceeded that from the west and north of the continent by 50 percent.

According to U.S. Immigration and Naturalization Service figures, over 36 million Europeans immigrated to the United States between 1820 and 1976. Here is the breakdown of countries from which the largest number of European immigrants have come:

Germany	6,960,000
Italy	5,278,000
Great Britain (England, Scotland, Wales)	4,863,000
Ireland	4,722,000
Austria and Hungary	4,313,000
Russia (U.S.S.R.)	3,362,000
Sweden	1,270,000
Norway	856,000
France	744,000
Greece	638,000

Other European countries from which substantial numbers of persons have immigrated to America include Portugal, Denmark, Netherlands,

Switzerland, Spain, Belgium, Romania, Czechoslovakia, Poland, Yugoslavia, and Bulgaria.

According to the 1990 census, the largest number of Americans, 58 million, trace their ancestry to Germany. Americans of Irish ancestry form the next largest group, 39 million, followed by 32 million who claim English ancestors.

In view of these figures, it would be more accurate to say that for much of our history we have been a nation of immigrants *from Europe.* But we would have to add—and *from Africa.* Over 30 million Americans today trace their ancestry to the African continent.

America's Love-Hate Relationship with Immigration

"IMMIGRATION is as American as apple pie."

That statement by an editorial page staff writer recently appeared in the nationally influential *Washington Post.* Without doubt millions of Americans, past and present, have agreed with and still agree with his statement. For almost a hundred years after nationhood, immigration into the United States was completely unrestricted; anyone who could buy a boat ticket or walk across the Mexican or Canadian border could come here to live. George Washington seemed to speak for the country when he said, "The bosom of America is open . . . to the oppressed and persecuted of all Nations and Religions."

A deep-rooted American belief is that much of our strength as a nation comes from our being a union of so many diverse cultures and races. In *The American Way of Life* Princeton University professor Ashley Montague wrote, " . . . there can be little doubt that a great part of the vitality which is so characteristic of the American scene is due to the static generated by so many different cultural charges."

While he was still a senator, John F. Kennedy wrote a book entitled *A Nation of Immigrants* in which he made clear his belief in a liberal immigration policy. Speaking of immigration, he said, " . . . it infused the nation with a commitment to far horizons and new frontiers, and thereby kept the pioneer spirit of American life, the spirit of equality and hope, always alive and strong."

These statements are generalizations of how immigration has played a crucial role in shaping the national character of the United States; adding specifics to the generalizations is not difficult. The ideas of human rights, representative democracy, and justice on which our Constitution is based were brought from England by immigrants. These ideas were added to (in part by examples of Native American tribal governments and alliances) and tested in America; but the framers of our Constitution were most familiar with British political theory and practice.

Our religions—except for Native American religions—were brought here by immigrants. Our traditions of religious freedom, tolerance, and separation of church and state were fostered by Protestants and Catholics who suffered religious persecution in Europe. Each successive wave of immigrants—English and Scotch, Germans, Scandinavians, Irish, Jews—contributed to their new homeland their cultural values and traditions, food, music, and above all determination to succeed in America. We are an English-speaking nation, but our language has been enriched by thousands of words from the Spanish, German, Italian, and French languages which were the mother tongues of immigrants to America.

The forced immigration of hundreds of thousands of Africans to America in the eighteenth and nineteenth centuries profoundly affected our history and national character. This immigration led to the nation's Civil War. It has kept questions of human dignity and civil rights in the forefront of our national thinking and conscience as the large

The Native American population of the United States has more than tripled in the past thirty years because hundreds of thousands of Americans who once hid their Indian roots have become proud of their Indian ancestry. Indian leaders, writers, and artists are making a major effort to acquaint other Americans with Indian history, culture, and contributions to our country. Scores of tribes hold powwows and cultural celebrations every year. The White Mountain Apaches of Arizona, shown above, welcome visitors to their reservation to share their dances, food, and crafts.

African-American minority has fought to take its rightful place in America.

But immigration has always had doubters and outright opponents, concerned about the numbers and nationalities of people coming to America. Even in colonial times, a quarter century before the signing of the Declaration of Independence, no less a founding father than Benjamin Franklin was demanding to know why German immigrants should " . . . be suffered to swarm into our Settlements, and by herding together, establish their Language and Manners, to the Exclusion of ours? Why should Pennsylvania, founded by the English, become a Colony of Aliens, who will shortly be so numerous as to Germanize us instead of our Anglifying them?"

By the mid-nineteenth century opponents of immigration were finding group voices loud enough to be clearly heard; this was particularly true in growing American cities where residents were concerned about the effect of immigrants on jobs and wage levels. The American Protective Association was formed to protest increasing Irish immigration. The Know-Nothings, a political movement of the 1840s and 1850s, resented the growth of Roman Catholic immigration in particular but were antagonistic to immigration in general; they advocated denying the rights of freeborn Americans to all immigrants, even those from England and other European countries.

In a letter written in 1855, Abraham Lincoln made clear how he felt about the Know-Nothing belief that constitutional rights should apply to some people while being denied to others. "As a nation we began by declaring that *all men are created equal*," Lincoln wrote. "We now practically read it *all men are created equal except negroes*. When the Know-Nothings get control, it will read *all men are created equal, except negroes, and foreigners, and Catholics*. When it comes to this I should prefer emigrating to some other country where they make no pretence of loving liberty—to Russia, for instance, where despotism can be taken pure, without the base alloy of hypocrisy."

Candle lighting at Kwanzaa, an African-American cultural celebration. The candles represent the seven principles on which Kwanzaa is based: unity, self-determination, collective work and responsibility, cooperative economics, purpose, creativity, faith. Kwanzaa is observed from December 26 through January 1. Kwanzaa comes from the Swahili word kwanza, *which means "the first" or "the first fruits of the harvest."*

During the mid-nineteenth century a small number of Chinese and Japanese began to arrive in California, primarily to become laborers on railroads being built in the American West. They also became farm laborers and worked in laundries, restaurants, and other service establishments in cities. Although their numbers were never large compared to European immigrants, the fear of a "Yellow Peril," of uncontrolled cheap labor and strange customs and religions, caused labor and other groups to press Congress for restrictions.

The result was the Chinese Exclusion Act of 1882. Despite its name, this law did not call for the deportation of Chinese already in the country, but it did shut off future immigration from China (except for

There are far more adherents of Christianity in the United States (almost 140 million) than of all other religions combined. But many other religions flourish and are freely practiced in America; Judaism has the second largest number (about 6 million), Islam the third largest (about 2.5 million). Several Buddhist sects in the United States total over 200,000 members. Shown here is the temple of the Buddhist Congregational Church of America in Washington, D.C. (Above figures are from the 1991 Universal Almanac.)

teachers, diplomats, and merchants). The Chinese Exclusion Act was the first piece of U.S. legislation restricting immigration, and, ominously, the restrictions were based on race and country of origin.

Encouraged by their success, restrictionists (persons favoring severe limits on immigration) persuaded Congress to expand the Chinese Expulsion Act by establishing an "Asiatic Barred Zone." The new law, passed in 1917, prohibited the immigration of laborers from China, India, Burma (Myanmar), Siam (Thailand), the Malay States, Asiatic Russia, and most Polynesian islands. An earlier "Gentleman's Agreement" between the United States and Japan prohibited the immigration of laborers from Japan.

But shutting off the small flow of Asians to America was only a secondary concern of immigration restrictionists. What really alarmed them was the pattern of immigration that developed between 1900 and 1909. If the flood of immigrants from Italy, Russia, and other southern and eastern European countries continued, they and their offspring might eventually outnumber persons of northern and western European ancestry.

Congress decided to act against that possibility. The Quota Act of 1921, given final form in the National Origins Act of 1924, put an annual limit of 150,000 immigrants from the Eastern Hemisphere. The new law set country quotas that were determined by the percentage of each nationality already in the United States according to the 1910 census. This quota system made certain that many more immigrants could come from northern and western Europe—Great Britain, Ireland, Germany, France, Netherlands, Scandinavia—than from southern and eastern Europe—countries such as Italy, Russia, and Greece. Under the National Origins Act, 82 percent of the total of 150,000 immigrants permitted annually went to countries of northern and western Europe and 16 percent to those of southern and eastern Europe. Only 2 percent was left for all of the other countries of the Eastern Hemisphere, including those of Africa. Almost all Asian immigration was prohibited by earlier laws.

The purpose of this highly discriminatory legislation was to preserve the "ethnic balance" of the United States as it was at that time. Most Americans in the 1920s—as is still the case today—could trace their ancestry to northern and western European countries. The quota system was developed to ensure that the United States would continue to have a majority with that ancestral background.

HARDLY had the nationality quota system gone into effect than immigration to America diminished to a trickle for other reasons. The Great Depression of the 1930s paralyzed the economy of the United

While ethnic festivals are increasingly popular in the United States, they have always been a part of American life. The above scene is the queen and her court in the Holy Ghost festival, a Portuguese-American celebration in Santa Clara, California, 1942.

States, stopping all business and industrial growth, depressing farm prices, throwing millions of people out of work. America was no longer seen as a land of opportunity. The whole world was in a depression. Many people who would have come to America despite the hard times were too poor to pay their passage. In the ten-year period between 1930 and 1939 only slightly more than half a million immigrants came to the United States, compared to an average of 6 million in each of the earlier decades of the century.

Immigration was also very sparse during the years of World War II, 1939–1945, which the United States entered in 1941. In 1943 only 23,700 immigrants came to America, the lowest immigration for any year since record keeping began in 1820.

During the depression and war years many government officials and migration specialists became convinced that the era of large-scale immigration to America was over.

22

An Immigration Law without Bigotry

BUT the experts were wrong. The United States emerged from World War II with unbounded energy, strength, and confidence. The nation's factories were producing at full capacity; the construction industry was booming; anyone who wanted a job could find one. In a world of war-shattered countries, millions of people dreamed once more of beginning a new life in America. After 1945, immigration to the United States quickly reached the annual limit set by the National Origins Act of 1924.

Before World War II the United States had embraced a philosophy of isolationism. The war brought the nation into a closer relationship with the rest of the world and changed the way Americans looked at other countries and people. After the war many Americans began to question the racism and prejudice against certain nationalities that had become a part of U.S. immigration policy.

The first four post-World War II U.S. presidents all favored passage of a new immigration law that did not discriminate against people on the basis of race, nationality, and religion. President Truman vetoed a 1952 immigration law because it continued country quotas for immigrants, but Congress passed the law over his veto. President Eisenhower urged changes in immigration law to "get the bigotry out of it." President Kennedy said that immigration quotas based on race and country of origin were "without basis in either logic or reason."

Because of the Vietnam War and the civil rights revolution spearheaded by African Americans, the 1960s were years of soul-searching for most Americans about social justice and human rights. In 1965 Congress passed and President Johnson signed into law a new immigration act which brought racial and ethnic quotas to an end. Although a number of changes have been made in the landmark 1965 law, it remains the basis for the present law. U.S. immigration law today is very complex with scores of provisions, but the main elements are these:

- No person can be refused immigrant status to the United States because of race, nationality, or religion.
- The annual limit on immigration is determined by Congress. The limit has risen steadily from the cap of 155,000 set by the 1924 law. The 1965 law raised the limit to 270,000. The annual immigrant ceiling was later raised to 500,000 and was raised to 700,000 in 1990.
- Minor children and parents of legal immigrants already residing in the country do not count against the regular immigration limit.
- Refugees from political or religious persecution who are admitted to the United States do not count against the regular immigration limit.
- Immigrants from any single country are limited to 20,000 per year, although Congress can adjust upward the figure for an individual country in special cases. Refugees do not count against the 20,000 per country limit.
- Preference in issuing immigrant visas will be shown for (1) family reunification—close relatives of U.S. citizens or legally resident noncitizens, (2) persons with special occupational and professional skills that will be useful in the United States.

The Immigration Act of 1965 once again opened the golden door that had been closed for forty years by racial and ethnic prejudice. Dramatic changes in immigration to America were about to begin.

2

Today's Immigrants

> "We grow up with the idea that America is a magic place. When we get here, we find out that what we believed is true. But you have to make the magic happen yourself, through hard work."
>
> Jamaican immigrant

Most of today's immigrants, like this Cambodian family arriving at Washington, D.C., National Airport, are met by relatives or sponsors.

"DETROIT is our Ellis Island."

I heard that statement frequently while I was interviewing Arab Americans in Detroit. I heard it from a young Palestinian woman whose parents had sent her to America to escape the tensions of living in the Israeli-occupied West Bank; from a Lebanese man who left Lebanon after his two brothers had been killed in the country's terrible civil war; from the owner of a bakery who had arrived in Detroit with less than ten dollars in his pocket. In each case their entry into the United States had been through the Detroit Metropolitan Airport. They were joining the 250,000 other Arab Americans who make the Detroit area their home.

Today most legal immigrants to the United States arrive at the country's great international airports in Miami, New York, Los Angeles, San Francisco, Houston, Chicago, Boston, and many other cities. These airports are their Ellis Islands, but their arrival in their new home bears faint resemblance to that of immigrants who sailed into New York

Harbor in the first years of this century. Those early immigrants might have stayed for days in the barracks at Ellis Island waiting to be interviewed, to have their papers checked—if they had papers—and to receive medical examinations. When they were finally released from the Ellis Island receiving center, most had to take a train or bus to wherever their home in the United States was to be.

Today's immigrants arrive with passports containing entry visas issued by the American embassy or consulate in the country they came from. Often immigration officials speak the immigrants' language, and usually the newcomers have their passports stamped and their baggage cleared through customs without delay.

Many immigrants arrive in the city where they expect to live. And most, when they emerge from immigration and customs into the airport's public area, find members of their family—a brother, sister, uncle, parent, son, or daughter who had already immigrated to America—waiting to greet them and make their adjustment to a new life in a strange land a little easier.

But it is still a strange land they have come to, most of them with little or no English and often with little knowledge of how things work in a highly industrialized country. I met several times with immigrant students in an English-as-a-second-language class at Annandale High School in Annandale, Virginia. Annandale is a suburb of Washington, D.C., and in recent years our nation's capital has become a major magnet for immigrants. The Annandale students were finishing their first semester in special English study and understood pretty well, but some were shy about using their new language. I got them to talk by going over some "Coming to America" experiences they had written for their teacher, Kathy Hermann. They seemed to find them amusing now, but I'm sure they weren't funny at the time.

A girl named Rania from the Middle East said, "The day we arrived my uncle took us to his house. I was thirsty, and he gave me a can of Coke, but I didn't know how to open it. He had to show me. Later I

Author Brent Ashabranner with a class at Annandale High School.

went into the kitchen to get water, but I didn't know how to turn the faucet on, and my aunt had to show me."

Osphea, a girl from Cambodia, told of her awe when she first saw an American kitchen—the gas stove, refrigerator, sink, and cabinets. But the bathroom inside the house astonished her most of all. "Always," she said, "in the country I came from the bathroom was outside."

A Korean boy talked about how lonely he had been when he first arrived, living in his uncle's house. One day he walked out on the street hoping to find a friend. "But everyone rode in cars," he said. "No one was walking, so I went back in the house." And he added, "I missed my friends in Korea."

But all of them, when I met them, were on their way to finding their places in their new country. The Korean boy said, "When I came to Annandale High School, I found friends. Best of all, I found a girlfriend."

Who Are the Newcomers?

THROUGHOUT the nineteenth century and well into the twentieth, over 80 percent of all immigrants to America came from Europe. Only 5 percent came from Latin America and not more than 3 percent came from Asia during that period. But after World War II, European immigration decreased sharply. With United States help the war-ravished countries of Western Europe recovered and became prosperous. Their well-off citizens had little incentive to emigrate. At the same time the Communist countries of Europe—Russia, Poland, Czechoslovakia, East Germany, and others—slammed the door on emigration, keeping their citizens locked behind the Iron Curtain.

Instead of decreasing, however, total immigration to the United States began a steady increase. The poor and overpopulated countries of Asia had been waiting for almost a hundred years for the golden door to America to open. When it did open in 1965, they came. With the fall of South Vietnam to the Communists in 1975, followed by fighting and chaos in Laos and Cambodia (Kampuchea), an outpouring of refugees greatly increased the number of Asians coming to the United States.

The countries of Latin America had never been under a U.S. immigration quota system (the quota system applied only to the Eastern Hemisphere) until 1965, but immigration was light from Hispanic countries until the mid-twentieth century. Then deteriorating economic conditions in some of the countries, political problems in others, plus increasingly easy international travel and communications brought about a rapid growth of Latin-American immigrants.

By the 1980s Europeans made up not 80 percent of the immigrants to American but just 13 percent. Instead of 8 percent, Asians and Latin Americans now made up 80 percent—about 40 percent from Asia, 40

Hispanic festivals such as this one in Herndon, Virginia, are widely held throughout the United States to celebrate the music, food, art, and other aspects of Latin-American culture. The Herndon festival featured Mexican mariachi music, a folk band, and folk songs. Musicians played instruments indigenous to Bolivia, El Salvador, Paraguay, Peru, and other Central and South American countries.

percent from Latin America. In only a few years the pattern of world-wide immigration to America was turned upside down.

A POPULATION census of the United States is taken in every year that ends in zero. The first census was taken in 1790 and has been taken every ten years since. In 1790 the total population of the United States was about 4 million. Two hundred years later, in 1990, it was just short of 250 million—a quarter of a billion people.

The census gives us a statistical picture of what we look like as a

31

nation. How many people who live in the United States are white? How many are black? How many are of Asian or Latin American origin? How many are American Indians? Where in the United States do all these people live? What kind of work do they do? The census answers these questions and many more. The census also tells us how we change as a nation from decade to decade. Here is some of the information that the 1990 census gave us about immigration and the growth of racial and ethnic minorities:

The country's population grew from 226.5 million in 1980 to 248.7 million in 1990. All growth comes either from natural increase (the surplus of births over deaths) or immigration. In the decade of the eighties, 28 percent of the growth came from immigration.

In the decade 1980–1989, 8.9 million legal immigrants came to America. This was the greatest influx of immigrants in any ten-year period in the nation's history. The old record was 8.8 million for the years 1900–1909.

The Asian population of the United States more than doubled, from 3.5 million in 1981 to 7.3 million in 1990—an increase of almost 108 percent. People of Chinese ancestry make up the largest segment of Asian Americans, followed by Filipinos, Japanese, Asian Indians, Koreans, and Vietnamese.

The Hispanic population rose from 14.6 million to 22.3 million—an increase of 53 percent. About half of the increase was from immigration. "Hispanic" is a term that includes people of Mexican, Puerto Rican, and Cuban origin, plus all others from Spanish-speaking countries of Latin America and Spain. Hispanics may be of any race.

African Americans continued to be the largest minority, growing from 26.5 million to 30 million. The rate of growth was 13.2 percent, and African Americans now make up 12.1 percent of the U.S. population. Not much of the growth in the decade of the eighties came from immigration, however. Africans today make up only about 3 percent of all immigrants to America.

"Cultural diversity—racial and ethnic diversity—accelerated more in the 1980s than in any other decade," says Carl Haub, senior demographer at the Population Reference Bureau in Washington, D.C., "even compared to the high immigration early in this century. Almost all of those immigrants were coming from just a few European countries. Now we've got people coming from all corners of the world."

Haub's statement made me think again about Annandale High School. The classes I had met with had students from Korea, El Salvador, Vietnam, Cambodia, Afghanistan, Peru, Iran, Pakistan, and Israel. But that was only part of the school's diversity story. I didn't visit all of the special English classes. There were also immigrant students from Colombia, Argentina, Bolivia, Venezuela, Honduras, Dominican Republic, Ethiopia, Poland, Turkey, India, Philippines, Indonesia, Jordan, Portugal, Sierra Leone, and Taiwan. Some of the students—such as those from India and the Philippines—already had good English skills and didn't need special help. But most did.

G. Raymond Watson, the Annandale High School principal, gave me some startling figures. Today his school has a 37 percent minority enrollment. He broke it down this way: 63 percent white, 20 percent Asian, 9 percent black, 8 percent Hispanic. The demographic forecast is that in a few years minority students will make up more than half of the student body.

"Ten years ago the minority figure was 11 percent," Ray Watson told me, "in the seventies a lot less than that. Now we've got the whole world in our classrooms!"

Why Do They Come?
New Faces, Old Hopes

WHY do people leave their homelands to come to America where, often for a long time, they struggle to learn a new language, new customs, unfamiliar technologies, adjust to new foods, new ways of looking at the world? Ashley Montague has this answer: "The first and the last of its immigrants have come to America in order to begin a new life. They left the old country for the new country in order to better themselves."

Without doubt Professor Montague is right. The hope of a better life surely has motivated almost all immigrants who have come to America. Of course, a better life means different things to different people. The Pilgrims who sailed from England and founded Plymouth Colony in 1620 did not expect an easier or economically richer life than they had in England; for them a better life meant the chance to practice their religion the way they wanted to. For tens of thousands of refugees from Vietnam and Cambodia, a better life in America simply meant escaping political oppression, prison, or death from a vengeful regime in their native lands.

But for the "huddled masses" who passed through Ellis Island or preceded or followed them, the hope of a better life in America meant the chance to earn a decent wage, to start a business or own a farm, to build or buy a house, to send their children to school—all dreams that could not come true in the old country they left behind. They believed those dreams could come true in America. To make them come true in a climate of political freedom: that was the American dream.

That remains the American dream for immigrants to this day. The faces have changed from those of Europeans to those mainly of Asians

Mario Casteneda

and Latin Americans, but the hopes and dreams are as old as the first immigrants who came to the New World.

The promise of the dream has always outweighed the fear of the unknown. That was true for Mario Casteneda. He was born in the Central-American country of El Salvador and lived the first twenty-four years of his life near the city of Usulutan. His parents farmed a small piece of land, but there was not nearly enough income, work, or food for the family that included six girls and four boys. Mario went to elementary school but had to drop out after that to try to earn a few pesos to contribute to the family income. He took any job he could find, sometimes working on other farms, sometimes selling trinkets on the streets of Usulutan, occasionally doing manual labor on roads. But most of the time he could find no work.

Many Salvadorans, caught in the bitter political civil war that consumed their country in the 1970s and 1980s, sought refuge in the United States. The fighting did not affect Mario or his family, but as he approached his twenty-fifth birthday, he decided he would never have a real job or make a real living unless he left El Salvador and went to the United States.

Mario's mother gave him her blessing to leave El Salvador; she also gave him one hundred dollars, all she received from selling her last piece of gold jewelry. With a brother-in-law who decided to leave, too, Mario traveled through Mexico by bus and reached Tijuana on the U.S.-Mexican border. They checked into a cheap hotel in Tijuana and paid their bill in advance—a wise move because before the day was out Mario discovered that his pocket had been picked. What remained of his one hundred dollars was gone.

The hotel owner connected Mario and his brother-in-law with a "coyote" who agreed to smuggle them across the border and take them to Los Angeles. A coyote is a person who guides or smuggles illegal aliens across the U.S.-Mexican border. Often coyotes are criminals who rob and abandon those they have agreed to help, but Mario and his companion were lucky. The coyote got them to Los Angeles and received five-hundred dollars in payment from another of Mario's brothers-in-law who lived there.

Mario worked at miscellaneous jobs in Los Angeles long enough to repay his brother-in-law and to learn some English in a church-run night class. Then he went to Washington, D.C., to live because a relative there told him the chances for work might be better. Wherever he was, Mario was always under the shadow of being an illegal alien; at any time he might have been caught by Immigration and Naturalization Service agents and sent back to El Salvador.

Again Mario was one of the lucky ones. In 1986 Congress passed a law setting big fines and even prison terms for U.S. employers who hire illegal aliens. The purpose of the law was to discourage illegal entry into the country by people wanting jobs. In the same law Congress extended amnesty to illegal aliens who had entered the United States before January 1, 1982, and had lived in the country continuously since that date. Such persons could file papers asking to become permanent legal residents of the United States. If approved, they would be issued a "green card" making their employment legal, and after five years they could apply for citizenship. Mario had reached Los Angeles in 1980. He was one of the 2.3 million illegal immigrants who applied for amnesty. He was approved and became a legal resident of the United States.

Mario has worked at many jobs in the Washington, D.C., area. His first job was as a busboy in a Greek restaurant. He has worked for landscaping firms, planting and maintaining lawns, trees, and shrubs. Mostly he has worked on construction jobs as a laborer, once being promoted to crew chief. He has spent chunks of time out of work and looking for work. With little education, no special skills, and halting English, his opportunities are severely limited; but he believes he is a good construction worker, and his one advancement to crew chief has given him hope.

Mario misses his family in El Salvador, and he misses the familiar life of that country. Although money is always a problem, he has managed to save enough to fly to Usulutan three times to see his family and friends.

I asked Mario if he thought he might someday return to Usulutan to stay, and he pondered his answer. "I do not think so," he said after some moments. "Where in El Salvador could I ever earn enough money to fly in an airplane?"

A great many immigrants like Mario live in the United States today, mostly in Los Angeles, New York, Chicago, Houston, and a few other big cities. Most, also like Mario, are without education or premium skills. Some eventually will prosper, at least modestly. Others will do fairly well when the U.S. economy flourishes, poorly when it does not. But few of those who do poorly will return to the country they came from, where even greater poverty would await them.

JOE MARTHA, a Palestinian, came to the United States for the simplest of reasons: His life in Ramallah, a city in the Israeli-occupied West Bank, was going nowhere, and he saw no chance that his fortunes would improve. Two of his brothers had already immigrated to America, and Joe followed them, helped in getting a visa by the family reunification preference of the immigration law. For Joe, like thousands of other Palestinians who have fled the turmoil and hopelessness of their situation in the Middle East, Detroit was his Ellis Island.

"I'm a hustler," Joe told me during one of our talks. "When I first came here I worked three jobs at a time."

He worked all day and often until midnight. Every morning he had to take four buses across Detroit to get to one place where he worked. He took service jobs, jobs in stores. Joe had a plan, a purpose behind his torrent of work. After the 1967 war between Israel and the Arabs, Joe began to use all the money he made, except the small amount he needed to live on, to bring his family and other close relatives to America.

Joe first brought over his parents, then three sisters. He kept at it over a number of years until sixteen of his relatives were living in America because of his efforts and financial help. After that Joe borrowed some money and started a "party store" (the local name for convenience store) in Monroe, a town near Detroit. With the help of his wife, Rozette, and the same kind of energy that he has always poured into his life in America, Joe has made a success of his store. Today he

Joe Martha serving dinner for his family. At the head of the table is one of his nieces that he helped come to the United States.

and Rozette live in a big, pleasant house not far from the store. The house is well filled with their four children and Joe's mother.

"I will never forget the country I came from," Joe said to me, "and I will never forget the opportunity I found in this country, which is now my country."

Joe Martha's efforts to bring his relatives to America is an example of what immigration specialists call "chain migration." A person immigrates to America, gets settled, and helps some member or members of his family come to this country. The newcomers, when they are established, help or encourage still other relatives to come. A family chain of immigrants is formed and grows. The family reunification preference of the immigration law helps the chain migration process.

Zahra Nikseresht

ZAHRA NIKSERESHT is Iranian. She lived in the city of Shiraz until she was nineteen; her father was and still is a successful physician there. Zahra went to an excellent private secondary school in Shiraz, receiving a good foundation in mathematics and chemistry. During the summers her father insisted that she enroll in classes in English.

After the Iranian revolution, Zahra's father decided that she should go to the United States for her university education, and Zahra agreed. Whether she would try to remain in the United States after she finished her education or return to Iran to live was something to be decided in the future. The United States does not have diplomatic relations with Iran, but Zahra was able to get a student visa from the American embassy in Turkey. She flew to Miami, where an older brother was already going to school, and enrolled at Miami-Dade Community College.

Almost everything about America agreed with Zahra. She bought a car, an old clunker but good enough to get her back and forth to class. She had no trouble getting a driver's license or driving in Miami. "I learned to drive in Shiraz," she said, "and after that Miami traffic was a piece of cake." Neither was she long in becoming comfortable with American slang.

Zahra did well in school, taking a two-year Associate of Arts degree in premed. After that she switched to the University of Florida in Gainesville; there was too much "partying" in Miami, she said, and she was serious about her education. She had come to the United States with the intention of becoming a doctor, like her father, but at Gainesville she decided that pursuing a medical degree was too long and expensive and unfair to her father. Finding U.S. dollars for her support was very difficult for him.

Her interest in medicine remained strong, however, and she decided to enroll in Florida Agricultural and Mechanical University's program in physical therapy. Florida A.&M. is one of the few schools that offers degree training in working with patients who have had strokes, spinal cord injuries, head injuries, and with children with cerebral palsy. Zahra quickly discovered that being admitted to Florida A.&M. was not going to be easy. It is a popular school in Florida, particularly for African Americans, and there was little or no room for foreigners.

But Zahra was persistent. She went to Tallahassee, where the university is located, and pleaded her case vigorously with admissions officials. "I love this country," she told them. "I want to stay here and be a part of it." Finally she was accepted.

Zahra has stayed here. She received her degree, applied for and

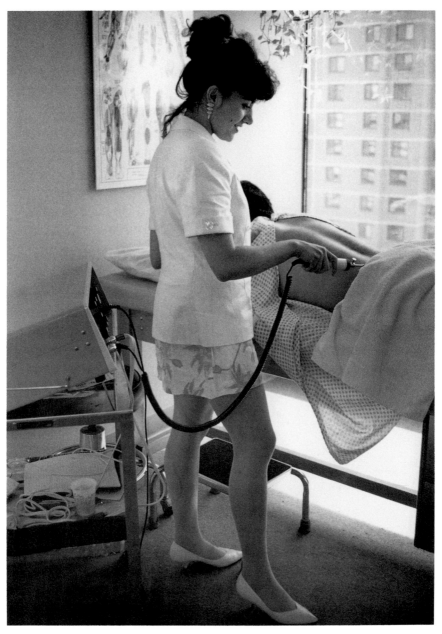

Zahra Nikseresht works hard as a therapist and is ambitious. In addition to her full-time job, she is taking courses at nearby George Mason University with the thought of someday going into sports medicine.

received permanent resident status, and is now working at the Rehabilitation Medicine Center of Northern Virginia. Zahra told me that she likes the "freedom" of America, the openness, the chances for upward movement.

"And," she said, "I like the way people mind their own business."

ROGER JANTIO, an immigrant born in the West African country of Cameroon, is a highly educated and well-traveled man. He has received graduate degrees in economics and finance in France and a master of business administration degree from the Harvard Business School. He now has started his own company to provide financial advisory services to African governments and corporations working in Africa. While acknowledging that most immigrants have problems of various kinds in America, Jantio recently told a *Washington Post* staff writer:

"But when all is said and done, there is no better place for the immigrants. And I'm saying it after I have seen a lot of the world."

The experiences of millions of immigrants like Mario Casteneda, Joe Martha, and Zahra Nikseresht support Mr. Jantio's statement.

Illegal Aliens: A Special Problem

THOUSANDS of people come to the United States each year with no passport or proper entry visa issued by the American embassy or consulate in the country they come from. In the language of the U.S. Immigration and Naturalization Service, they are "undocumented." They are illegal aliens. Almost without exception they are people who would have no chance of being approved to immigrate to the United States or would have to wait years for approval.

Many illegal aliens come to the United States with the intention of

In times of labor shortage in the United States, Mexicans have been encouraged to work in this country. During World War II and for twenty years after the war ended, almost 5 million Mexican men, like those shown here, crossed the border to work temporarily on U.S. farms. They came under an agreement called the bracero *program, between the U.S. and Mexican governments. Millions of today's illegal immigrants are following in the footsteps of their* bracero *fathers who came legally.*

staying permanently; others plan to return to their home country after they have earned and saved some money, but often they decide not to return. Still others come to the United States to make money to send back to desperately poor families; they have no idea when or if they will return. Regardless of plans or motives, these illegal aliens are subject to immediate deportation if caught by the INS.

Some foreigners enter the United States legally with tourist or student visas but stay after their temporary visas have expired. Whatever their original intention might have been, they become illegal aliens. If they get into trouble with the law, they will be deported. Otherwise they are not likely to be caught because the INS does not have the manpower or money to hunt for them.

Accurate figures on illegal aliens are impossible to obtain for the simple reason that persons living in the United States illegally do not want to be counted. Enough is known about numbers, however, to make the problem of illegal aliens both bewildering and disturbing.

The 1990 census identified about 2 million adults and children as being in the country illegally, but other government and university studies suggest that the total may be much higher—3 million to 6 million. Estimates of the number of new illegal aliens coming into the United States annually with the intention of staying indefinitely range from 100,000 to 300,000.

The concentration of illegal aliens in certain urban areas causes special difficulties. Cities presently having an estimated 200,000 to 500,000 or more illegal aliens are Los Angeles, New York, Houston, Chicago, Miami, San Antonio, Newark, San Francisco, and San Diego. Most illegal aliens are poor, and many do not have occupational skills or much education. Their high concentration in a few urban locations causes problems of housing, education, health, unemployment, and crime.

About half of all illegal immigrants in the United States are visa abusers. The other 50 percent of illegal immigrants are undocumented persons who slip into the United States without visas or other immigrant papers. Some arrive by boat, some even by airplane, but overwhelmingly undocumented persons try to enter the United States by crossing our border with Mexico. In recent years the Border Patrol, according to INS figures, has apprehended about 1 million illegal aliens annually who have entered the United States by crossing the Mexican border. No one knows how many thousands or hundreds of thousands successfully avoided the Border Patrol. We do know from census and other studies that 55 to 60 percent of all illegal immigrants in the United States are Mexicans.

We know something else: no other international border is like the U.S-Mexican border. Nowhere else on earth does a rich highly industrialized country share such a long, open, easily crossed border with a large, poor, less-developed country. The border stretches for 1,952 miles from the Pacific Ocean near San Diego, California, to the Gulf of Mexico at Brownsville, Texas. The Rio Grande forms the border in Texas, but only a barbed-wire fence—fallen down in many places—defines most of its length across New Mexico, Arizona, and California. There are a number of favorite places for illegal entry, but places where determined undocumented aliens can cross the border are almost unlimited.

Without question the San Diego area is the most popular. San Diego and the Mexican border city of Tijuana, just thirteen miles away, are powerful people magnets. They are the gateway to California with its thousands of service jobs in motels, hotels, and restaurants and more thousands in the state's vast agricultural industry. The San Diego Border Patrol Sector shares sixty-six miles of border with the Mexican state of Baja California. Every night hundreds and often thousands of illegals pour across the border in this sector, and the Border Patrol tries to catch them. An astonishing 35 percent of all illegal aliens arrested along the entire U.S.-Mexican border are apprehended in the San Diego sector. But many are not caught.

One evening an hour before dark I rode through the San Diego sector with Supervisory Border Patrol Agent R. J. Miller. He drove his Ram Charger expertly along the rutted dirt tracks that parallel the border. We skirted the edge of steep, brush-filled canyons and stopped occasionally to look across into Mexico. The border fence, chain link in this sector, was less than a third of a mile away. Through field glasses we could see people on the Mexican side bunched up near the fence. They were every place we looked. In a flat area near Tijuana that the Border Patrol calls "the soccer field" a hundred or more people were standing around. By nightfall, Bob Miller said, there would be two or

A Border Patrol agent talks with two Guatemalans who have just been apprehended crossing the border into San Diego County.

three thousand waiting to come through the canyons and have their try at crossing the border.

"We'll be waiting for them," Miller said.

And they were. We stopped and chatted with several Border Patrol agents stationed along the edge of the canyons. "But you can't stop the tide," one of them said to me. "Not with a few men and a couple of choppers."

On another evening just before sunset I walked the sand hills near El Paso with Senior Border Patrol Agent H. M. "Mike" Calvert. El Paso with a population of 600,000 is the largest U.S. city directly on the Mexican border. Like San Diego, it is a magnet for illegals, but here in the desolate hills that stretch southward into Mexico, we saw no one on this day.

"How do you ever catch anyone out here?" I asked Mike.

"We've learned to do what the Indians used to do," Mike said. "We cut sign. If I see a cigarette butt or an empty tomato can or a candy wrapper, I start looking. This sand holds footprints real well, and I look for those. We have sensors buried in the trails. If someone steps on one, a signal goes off at headquarters, and I get a radio message."

I thought about the people Mike and I had seen earlier in the day waiting patiently on the Mexico side of the Rio Grande for night to come. At that time of year the river was hardly more than knee deep, and they would wade across. I thought about the thousands of illegals who were waiting along the two-thousand-mile border to cross that night.

"What is the answer?" I asked. I was really talking to myself, but Mike knew what I was talking about.

"If anyone knows, I haven't heard it," Mike said, but after a while he added, "Ninety-five out of a hundred of these illegals aren't bad people. They just want one thing—to get a job, work hard, and send money home to help their poor families. If they could make a decent living in Mexico, there wouldn't be any illegal alien problem, at least not much of one."

Since 1982 Mexico has been in a severe economic slump caused by falling oil prices. Millions of Mexicans are unemployed or underemployed. The falling value of the peso has made farming a starvation business. In addition, Mexico has a booming population, with almost a million young men and women entering the job market every year. For many who have lost their jobs, who have never had a job, or who cannot make a living farming, the only alternative is to try to come to the United States and find work.

The Immigration Control and Reform Act of 1986, which makes the hiring of illegal aliens by U.S. employers a crime, reduced the flow of illegal border crossers at first; but by 1991, the yearly border arrests had again risen to 1.2 million, 95 percent Mexicans.

They come despite the law prohibiting the hiring of illegals. Some find low-wage jobs in underground sweatshop industries where employers are willing to take the risk of hiring illegals in order to get cheap labor. Some illegals purchase forged documents and use them to convince employers that they are legal residents. Other illegal aliens live on charity from churches and other private civic organizations (not government welfare), through crime, or are supported by relatives living legally in the United States.

Some extremists would like to see a wall, like the Berlin Wall, built along the two thousand miles of our border with Mexico; a few have advocated using the army to patrol the entire length of the border. Polls have shown, however, that Americans overwhelmingly reject such police state measures.

Mike Calvert is right, of course. If Mexicans could find work in Mexico, most of them would never cross the border. Can the United States help Mexico solve its economic problems? Why should we try to do that when we can't solve our own economic problems? Surely, many people argue, the United States can't be expected to remedy the failure of all other countries to meet the needs of their poor. Indeed, we cannot, but Mexico is not just any other country.

"If the United States has one truly special relationship with another country, that country is Mexico," says William D. Rogers, former assistant secretary of state for Latin-American affairs. "A nation can choose its friends, but not its neighbors. We and Mexico are fated to live together. . . . We had best learn to exist side by side, with civility and understanding. What injures Mexico does damage to our own national interests as well."

But a sovereign nation must try to control its borders. So in the meantime, as we hope for and help with economic improvement in Mexico, the Border Patrol will do its best to stop the tide.

Amerasians: Coming Home?

AMONG the tragic legacies of the war in Vietnam are thousands of half-American children who were left in that country when the U.S. military effort ended there in 1975. They are the children of American servicemen or civilian workers and Vietnamese women. In some cases their fathers were killed in the war. In most cases the fathers simply returned to the United States at the end of their tour of duty and lost all contact with the mothers of their children and with the children themselves. Sometimes they never knew that they left children behind.

These children of American fathers and Vietnamese mothers grew up in a climate of scorn and hate. In Vietnam they were called *bui doi*, the "dust of life." As reminders of a hated enemy, they were considered worthless by most Vietnamese. Many were put into substandard orphanages. Some survived on city streets, living by their wits. Even those who had some semblance of a normal life with their mothers or relatives were frequently discriminated against in school and made fun of by other children.

The existence of thousands of half-American children was always well known to the U.S. defense and state departments and to Congress. For years following the U.S. military departure from Vietnam, however, almost nothing was done to try to bring at least some of the Amerasian children to America. It was as if, by ignoring them, the U.S. government could pretend they did not exist.

In 1979, through the efforts of the United Nations, Vietnam established an Orderly Departure Program which enabled some Vietnamese to apply for immigration to other countries. In 1982 Congress passed legislation giving Amerasian children immigrant status, but the law required the Amerasian child to come alone and live with foster parents in the United States. The Vietnamese mother could not accompany her child. Under this cruel restriction, the law was of benefit mainly to Amerasian orphans, although some Vietnamese mothers gave up their children in the hope that they would have a better life in America. Even with its restriction, more than four thousand Amerasian children came to the United Staes to live with foster parents.

With the Amerasian Homecoming Act of 1987, Congress at last authorized immigrant status not only for Amerasians but also for their immediate relatives: mothers, minor brothers and sisters, stepfathers. This humane piece of legislation was mainly the work of New York Congressman Robert Mrazek. Students at a school in Huntington, New York, had seen a newspaper picture of an Amerasian boy begging on the streets of Ho Chi Minh City (formerly Saigon). They wrote Mrazek urging him to help the boy and other Amerasians, and the congressman responded. He went to Vietnam, had face-to-face talks with Vietnamese officials, and brought back the Amerasian boy about whom the Huntington students had appealed to him. He then got congressional support for the Amerasian Homecoming Act, which quite properly is often referred to as the Mrazek Bill. The bill does not provide any direct financial assistance to Amerasian families coming to the United States; but, through volunteer assistance organizations, it does provide for initial housing, food, clothing, community orientation, medical care, and help with finding jobs.

Under the Mzarek Bill about 15,000 Amerasians and 35,000 members of their immediate families have come to America. An estimated 40,000 Amerasians and eligible family members remain in Vietnam;

Thuy with her husband, daughter, and mother.

how many of those will eventually come to the United States is unknown. Most Vietnamese Amerasians are now in their late teens or twenties, since few were born after 1975 and none after 1976.

Huynh Thi Diem Thuy (pronounced Twee) is twenty-nine and typical of many Amerasians now coming to America with their families. Thuy was born in Saigon in 1963, and her American father returned to the United States a year later. Thuy's mother, Huynh Thi Be (pronounced Bey), lived with Thuy's father for a year. He wrote to Be after he returned to America and sent pictures. But when the Communist North Vietnamese captured Saigon in 1975, Be burned all of the letters and pictures. Although Thuy has no memory of her father and no idea of what he looks like, she harbors a hope that she will meet him someday. That is unlikely, however. Letters stopped coming from him soon after the Communists took over Saigon, and Be cannot now remember his last name.

Life was hard in Ho Chi Minh City, but Be managed to keep her daughter and herself alive by selling cigarettes and sodas on the streets and by taking in sewing. Thuy was able to attend school for seven years, enduring the taunts of her classmates because she was *bui doi*, looked different, and was much taller than anyone her age.

Thuy applied for permission to come to America in 1982, when she was nineteen, but she got nowhere with the Vietnamese red tape. She kept trying but always with the same negative result. Thuy tried to find a job in Ho Chi Minh City, but because she was Amerasian no one would hire her; she learned sewing from her mother and made a little money that way. In 1985 she married Nguyen Duy Linh, and the following year their daughter Quyuh Anh was born. Linh, an electrician, was sometimes employed by the city's public works department.

When the Amerasian Homecoming Act became law, Thuy vigorously renewed her efforts to come to America. Her strongest reason for wanting to leave Vietnam was that she knew Quyuh Anh, as the daughter of an Amerasian *bui doi*, would also face lifelong prejudice. Finally, after nearly four years, Thuy's determination was rewarded; she and her whole family—husband, daughter, mother—were approved for immigration to the United States. In 1991, just twenty days before Christmas, they arrived in Washington, D.C.

Their adjustment to life in America is moving forward satisfactorily. They live in a part of the Virginia suburbs where a number of other Amerasian families have been settled. Their apartment is small but pleasant and adequately furnished. The family is Buddhist, and a small household shrine sits on a table in the living room; Be sees that a vase of fresh flowers is always on the table.

Linh and Be work at a nearby McDonald's. Linh hopes someday to work as an electrician, but he knows that he first must learn English and meet the requirements of the electrician's trade in America. That will take a long time. Thuy is pregnant again and not working, but she goes every day to English-as-a-second-language class. Quyuh Anh has started school and is receiving special help in English.

Quyah Anh. Children become immigrants because their parents are immi-grants. The children usually find learning to speak, read, and write English and absorbing American ways easier tasks than do their parents.

Thuy is very clear about her hopes for the future. She wants to learn English well and learn a skilled trade. She want Quyuh Anh and the child on the way to get a good education. She wants to become an American citizen.

"Already," Thuy will remind you with a smile that perhaps seems a bit sad, "I am half American. I want to be all American."

Who Are Refugees?
How Many Can the United States Take?

AMERICA has always been a haven for persons persecuted because of their political or religious beliefs. The Pilgrims were the first refugees to reach these shores. Since that time, millions have come to this country to escape tyranny and to be free to live according to their beliefs.

Throughout the middle part of the twentieth century, refugee status was reserved almost entirely for persons fleeing from Communist countries and for Palestinians escaping the conflicts and tensions of the Middle East. In 1980, however, Congress passed a law which defined a refugee as a person "who is unable or unwilling . . . to return to his country because of persecution on account of race, religion, or political opinion." Under this law, people anywhere in the world who are persecuted for political or religious reasons can ask to be admitted to the United States.

People admitted as refugees usually are given permanent resident status just as if they were regular immigrants. That is not always the case, however. During the years of political conflict in El Salvador, many Salvadorans came to the United States. The INS granted them asylum but not refugee status. If the political situation that caused their flight ended, asylum would be canceled and they would have to return to El Salvador.

The fighting that cost an estimated 75,000 lives finally was resolved in El Salvador, and asylum for Salvadorans in this country has been withdrawn by the INS. Many Salvadorans have been in the United States for years under the asylum decree; they have bought homes, started businesses, have children in school. They do not want to go back to El Salvador. Should they be made to go back? The problem is

Boat people. These Vietnamese refugees adrift in the South China Sea were rescued and taken to a refugee camp.

a difficult one; the INS has extended the Salvadorans' stay in this country while their fate is given further study.

The collapse of the Soviet Union has greatly reduced the number of people who might try to escape Communist regimes for political reasons; nevertheless, the world of today remains one of political and economic turmoil. The United Nations High Commissioner for Refugees estimates that the number of refugees in the world in 1992 is over 17 million. Millions of Africans are living outside their countries as refugees to escape ancient tribal hatreds and other political strife. Thousands of Vietnamese, Cambodians, and Laotians remain in refugee camps, and large numbers of Palestinians continue to live as refugees. In our hemisphere political tensions continue to erupt into violence in

Central America, and people still escape from Cuba, one of the few remaining Communist countries in the world.

How many of the world's refugees can the United States take for permanent settlement? Congress pondered that question, and the 1980 law specifies that the number of refugees entering the United States in any one year will be limited to 50,000. However, the law allows the president to admit an unlimited additional number of refugees if he believes that action is necessary. The president's only obligation is to advise and consult Congress if he increases the refugee limit. Perhaps it is not surprising that the president has increased the limit in every year since the refugee law was passed. In 1991, 100,000 refugees were admitted to the United States, and the number increased to 114,000 in 1992.

The flow of refugees from distant parts of the world can be controlled since few can reach the United States without the help of the U.S. government. But refugees from nearby countries such as El Salvador, Guatemala, Nicaragua, Cuba, and Haiti are quite a different matter. They can and do enter the United States by way of Mexico or by making a short sea voyage. In 1980 over 120,000 Cubans reached the shores of Florida in small boats; they were called Marielitos because they left from the Cuban port of Mariel.

During 1991 and 1992 thousands of Haitians risked death by leaving their country in small, often unseaworthy boats to try to reach the United States. Haiti is the poorest country in the Western Hemisphere and is in a state of anarchy. President Bush decided that the Haitians were not refugees, that they were not leaving Haiti because of political or religious persecution but because of the poverty and economic chaos there. The U.S. Coast Guard intercepted Haitian boats and turned them back to ports in Haiti; in some cases the Haitian boat people were put in makeshift camps, to be returned to Haiti as quickly as possible. A few have been admitted to the United States as refugees.

Even with the most liberal immigration and refugee policies, the

A Haitian refugee in Miami.

Left: Guatemalan refugees line up for food at a refugee camp in Mexico.

United States can take but a small percentage of the people who want, sometimes desperately, to come to this country. Distinguishing between true refugees—people who face persecution because of their political or religious beliefs—and those who are trying to escape wretched poverty is both painful and difficult today and is likely to become more difficult in the future.

A few years ago I interviewed a Haitian who was in this country illegally and working in the Florida sugarcane fields. He told me he was sending money home regularly; his wife had written him that their children were healthier than they had ever been.

This man from Haiti said to me, "People have told me that if the immigration puts me in a detention camp, I must say that I am a refugee. I tell them I do not know what a refugee is. They say a refugee is someone who has fled from his country because he was afraid the government would kill him or put him in prison because they do not like the way he thinks. I do not know about things like that. I left my country because if I did not come here my children would starve, and my government did not care whether they starved or not. I am a refugee from hunger."

3

What Today's Immigrants Bring to America

" . . . by any economic calculus, their hard work adds far more to the nation's wealth than the resources they drain."

From a *BusinessWeek* cover story
about today's immigrants

In 1943, a Portuguese-American couple making sausage. Ethnic foods have long added variety and tastiness to the U.S. diet.

AS WE have already seen, much goodwill toward immigrants has always existed in America; as we also have noted, the goodwill has been persistently tempered by a core of opposition and suspicion. Today is no different from the past. An editorial in a recent issue of the *Washington Post* is entitled "Needed: More Immigrants." A columnist in the Tucson, Arizona, *Star* writes, "Hail yesterday's immigrants. Today's. And tomorrow's. Our latest round of immigrant bashing turns my stomach." And in 1991 the president signed into law a bill increasing the number of immigrants who legally can come to America.

But as the country struggles with economic hard times, many Americans have negative feelings about immigrants and believe that Congress should not raise the ceiling on immigration. A public opinion poll conducted by the *New York Times* and CBS News recently showed that 49 percent of the people asked (a sample of 1,618 adults) felt that immigration should be decreased.

A poll conducted by the *Los Angeles Times* in 1988 asked this question: "Generally speaking, would you agree that immigrants in the past ten years have made a contribution to our country by enriching our culture, or disagree?" Forty-six percent of the 1,418 respondents said they believed immigrants had not enriched the culture. Sixty-four percent of the persons polled felt that immigrants take more from the economy in unemployment benefits and social services than they give in taxes and work.

Negative responses in polls such as these probably indicate a displeasure with and uneasiness about the general economic health of our country more than they do a specific unhappiness with immigrants, who are an easy target. Similar polls conducted in better economic times have shown positive feelings about immigrants.

Nevertheless, the high level of immigration today does present problems and challenges. The burdens of schools with special English language teaching and teaching students with a limited command of English are very real. Real also are the problems of our cities and states that receive a disproportionate share of new immigrants. Two-thirds of all newly arrived immigrants live in just five states: California, Texas, New York, Florida, and Illinois. These immigrants concentrate in the cities of those states, putting a strain on both state and city budgets for education and other social services.

A number of other cities such as Seattle, Minneapolis, and Washington, D.C., have similar problems, but there is nothing new about large numbers of immigrants settling in American cities. A look at history tells us that, by 1910, 75 percent of the residents of New York, Chicago, Detroit, Cleveland, and Boston were immigrants or their children. The cities of that era adjusted with some success to rapid multiethnic growth.

New Blood for Cities

IS AN influx of immigrants to the cities today necessarily bad? During the last decade millions of city residents left for the suburbs and smaller towns. Calculations by the magazine *BusinessWeek*, using census data, show that the ten largest American cities grew by 4.7 percent during the decade of the eighties, but without immigrants during that period their population would have shrunk by 6.8 percent. There would have been fewer people to buy merchandise in the stores, fewer people to pay taxes, fewer people to start new businesses. Without people, cities become hollow shells, as America knows very well.

Immigrants have revitalized areas of some cities that were badly rundown, sometimes in a state of decay. *BusinessWeek* gives the example of the Jefferson Boulevard area of south Dallas that it called "a dying inner-city business district." Ten years ago it was full of empty, boarded-up stores. Today it has new life with almost eight hundred businesses, three-fourths of them started by first- and second-generation immigrants. *BusinessWeek* quotes Leonel Ramos, Jefferson Area Association president, as saying, "They were hungry enough to start their own businesses."

Dallas is by no means a unique case. Elizabeth Bogen, director of New York City's office of immigrant affairs, has said that the influence of new immigrants was "unquestionably" favorable and that they have "revitalized declining neighborhoods." According to the *New York Times* immigrants in other cities have been praised as stabilizing, family-oriented forces in their communities. The *Times* cites nearby Jersey City as an example, where about fifteen thousand middle-class immigrants from India have settled. Jersey City officials say that the children of the Indian newcomers stay away from drugs and are seldom involved in any delinquent behavior.

Perhaps no American city has been more affected by immigrants in

Three young African Americans enjoy the Kunta Kinte Commemoration and Heritage Festival in Annapolis, Maryland. The festival, which has been held annually for several years, is named for Kunta Kinte, ancestor of famous African-American author Alex Haley (Roots). The festival pays tribute to the African American creative spirit with music and dance. African and African-American clothes, literature, and art are offered for sale.

recent years than Miami. In the early sixties thousands of Cubans fleeing the Communist regime of Fidel Castro made Miami their city of refuge. Many of these new arrivals were upper- and middle-class professional people—doctors, lawyers, college professors, bankers, business managers—who had opposed the dictator Fulgencio Batista as well as Castro who replaced him. Although most of them arrived penniless, they had the education, experience, and determination to succeed.

And succeed they did. By the 1980s the Cubans were a well-established and important part of Miami and south Florida life. An impressive number of Cuban doctors and lawyers are in practice. More than three thousand Cuban-owned businesses include construction companies, restaurants, boat companies, and shoe and clothing factories. Miami has several Cuban-owned or controlled banks.

The Spanish-language *Diario Las Americas* is a major Miami newspaper, and several Spanish-language television and radio stations are on the air. The highest-rated radio station in the Miami area broadcasts entirely in Spanish. As a result of the strong Cuban presence and Spanish language influence in Miami, the city has become a major shopping center for Latin America, with tourists coming from all over South and Central America. Miami Chamber of Commerce estimates are that in 1991 Latin American tourists spent $1.7 billion in Miami and south Florida.

Washington, D.C., is the fifth-ranking U.S. city in immigrant growth during the eighties. Census figures show that the foreign-born of the metropolitan area, which includes the suburbs, have passed half a million and make up about 14 percent of the total population. They have come from everywhere: Asia, Central America, South America, Africa, the West Indies, the Middle East.

Thousands of small businesses have sprung up as if by magic all over Washington and the suburbs. On Capitol Hill, our nation's capitol is ringed by small restaurants and cafes with names like Bangkok Orchid, Istanbul Cafe, Las Placitas (Salvadoran), Tortilla Coast, Thai

Roma (imagine Thai pizza!), and Suchiro (Japanese). Other kinds of small immigrant-owned businesses abound: grocery stores, tailor shops, dry cleaners, flower shops, and scores of sidewalk vendors offering jewelry, umbrellas, sandals, watches, and all kinds of exotic goods from around the world.

Today Washington pulses not only with Democratic and Republican politics but also with the energy of half a million immigrants.

Not Your Huddled Masses Anymore

MOHAMMAD AKHTER was born and grew up in a village in the Asian country of Pakistan, one of seven children in a large and poor family. He struggled to stay in school, went to college, and finally earned a medical degree. "I had to borrow a coat for graduation ceremonies," he told me. "I was that poor."

He managed to go to England to continue his studies; at first he worked as a grocery clerk because he was not licensed to practice medicine in Great Britain. Dr. Akhter came to the United States in 1970 after marrying an American woman—also a physician—while they were both at the University of Glasgow in Scotland. Dr. Akhter received additional training at the University of California, Johns Hopkins University, and the City University of New York.

Dr. Akhter has had a varied medical career. Among other positions, he spent several years as chief of emergency medical services for the state of Missouri. During the early 1970s, when the Vietnam War caused a shortage of physicians on American Indian reservations, Dr. Akhter and his wife volunteered some of their time to work on the Mescalero Apache and Navajo reservations in New Mexico and Arizona. Although

Dr. Mohammad Akhter.

Dr. Akhter is Muslim, he and his wife spent several years in Pakistan working as United Methodist Church medical missionaries.

Since returning from Pakistan, Dr. Akhter has become commissioner of health for the District of Columbia, the highest medical position in our nation's capital.

Sometimes his duties take him to a school in a depressed area of Washington, where most of the students are from families engulfed by urban poverty. "When I look at them," he said to me, "I can see myself as a boy, how I was then. And I want to say to them, 'If I did it, if I made something of my life, so can you.' "

Cavit Ayfer Durukan.

After a moment he added, "This country still provides the best opportunity to make something of yourself." Dr. Akhter was talking about native-born Americans as well as immigrants.

CAVIT AYFER DURUKAN is an immigrant from Turkey. He was born in the city of Bolu, where his father was a famous chef. From the time Cavit was nine years old, he helped his father in restaurant kitchens. Cavit left Turkey when he was twenty-one and spent several years studying cooking and working in Turkish and French restaurants in Switzerland, France, and England.

In 1986 Cavit came to the United States. He worked in restaurants in the Washington, D.C., area, including an excellent Turkish restaurant in Northern Virginia. After a few years he had an opportunity, in partnership with a Turkish friend, to start his own restaurant, the Istanbul Cafe, on Capitol Hill in Washington. The new restaurant, with Cavit as head chef, is drawing rave reviews from Washington gourmets.

"In America," says Cavit, "there is so much opportunity."

In Cavit's case—like so many immigrants today—he brought with him the training and experience to take advantage of opportunity when it came.

WASFY SHINDY is an immigrant from Egypt. While he was working toward his Ph.D. degree in agricultural chemistry at the University of California, he and his wife, who also is Egyptian, decided that they wanted to stay permanently in America. "In Egypt, with my Ph.D. from the University of California, I would have been a big fish," Dr. Shindy told me as I talked with him and his family one night in their nice suburban Los Angeles home. "Here in America I'm a small fish in a big tank. But I liked America, and we decided that our children would have a better future here than they would in Egypt. So we stayed."

Dr. Shindy is perhaps modest in calling himself a small fish. Today, as chief of the Los Angeles environmental toxicology laboratory, he is directly concerned with the health of all the residents of Los Angeles County.

HORATIO LOTUACO was born and raised in the Philippines. He earned a degree in chemical engineering at the University of Santo Tomas in Manila, worked at a sugar refinery in a provincial town and then as a technical sales representative for a chemical company in Manila. He did well, made good money, had personal use of a company car. But Horatio also had a taste for adventure, and slowly the idea of going to America and seeking his fortune there took root in his mind. Finally, he applied for a visa at the American embassy in Manila. Because of his training and experience as a chemical engineer, he did not have to wait long for immigrant status. Within three months after arriving in the United States, Horatio had a job—working for a sugar refinery in Baltimore. From that beginning in his new country, Horatio has gone on to earn a master's degree in business administration and is now systems analyst for Anne Arundel County schools in Maryland.

Violeta Lotuaco, like her husband Horatio, was born in the Philippines and went to school there, taking a degree in economics from the University of Santo Tomas. Although she and Horatio went to the same university in Manila, they did not meet until she immigrated to the United States and settled in Washington, D.C. Violeta worked for twenty years for the International Monetary Fund in Washington, but a few years ago she resigned.

"I decided it was time to follow my dream," she told me.

Her dream was to start and build her own business. Using her knowledge of the international community in the nation's capital and its suburbs, Violeta built a successful travel and real estate agency in Bethesda, Maryland. She is now well into her most ambitious and exciting project: a joint venture with a Philippine development corporation to market vacation-retirement villas in the Philippines for Fil-

Violeta Lotuaco in her Alpha Travel Agency office.

ipino Americans who want a "home away from home" in the land of their birth.

GEORGE AGUILAR has enough energy for two people, maybe three, and his energy has always had a rich mixture of ambition. He was born in Lima, Peru, and embarked on a college law program when he was eighteen. He studied for six years, and, while he was still in school, served as legal assistant to his lawyer uncle. Before graduating, however, George became a labor relations executive in a shoe manufacturing company. Still in a hurry, he decided to start his own company, manufacturing athletic shoes, and was able to get the necessary financial backing. For a time business boomed, but then a combination of moving too fast and bad financial times in Peru forced him to suspend operations and left him in debt.

George Aguilar.

"It was then that I decided to come to the United States," George told me. "I could think of no other way to make enough money quickly so that I could pay my debts and save my shoe business."

He arrived in the United States in 1983, sponsored by his uncle who had immigrated to America and was practicing law in Virginia. But George discovered soon enough that making money fast was an immigrant dream rather than reality. He had education and business experience, but he knew nothing about the United States, had no money, knew no English. His beginnings in his new country were much the same as millions of other immigrants. He studied English, he worked in restaurants, sometimes two in the same day. He worked on construction jobs during the day and at restaurants at night.

The Aguilar family. Virginia Aguilar has just become a U.S. citizen. The children are citizens because they were born in the United States. George Aguilar expects to become a citizen in the not-too-distant future.

Always the entrepreneur, he became a contractor and succeeded in getting some construction contracts, but lack of capital limited his success. He had much more success when in 1987 he saw that many immigrants needed help in filling out and filing papers under the new amnesty law for illegal aliens. Now his legal background, his Spanish, and his knowledge of Latin Americans became a great asset. He went into business helping amnesty seekers with the paperwork.

That successful undertaking led George to the discovery that many Latin American immigrants also need special help in making out federal and state income tax returns. He studied the income tax laws and went into that business, at which he is doing well today.

George Aguilar has been in the United States for ten years now, and thoughts of someday returning to Peru to live are receding. He married several years ago, and his wife, Virginia, a native of El Salvador, has recently become an American citizen. Their three children are already American citizens since they were born in the United States. "It seems that I will be next," George said.

His mind and his energy are always going strong. He has taken tests for entering law school. Going to law classes at night and working on tax cases during the day will not be easy, but George has never taken the easy way. He likes the idea of practicing law in the United States very much.

MOHAMMAD Akhter, Cavit Ayfer Durukan, Wasfy Shindy, Horatio and Violeta Lotuaco, and George Aguilar are illustrative of the many thousands of immigrants who now arrive in America every year with the education and experience to quickly adjust to their new homeland and make a useful contribution with minimum delay. During the decade of the 1980s over 1.5 million college-educated immigrants came to the United States, more than in any previous ten-year period. A recent study of employed immigrants for the period 1986–88 revealed that immigrants from India, the Philippines, China (Taiwan and mainland China

Thousands of immigrants come to the United States because they have married Americans. Nhung (Nan) Caristo met her husband when he was an officer in Vietnam. Like most other immigrants, Nan has brought the work ethic with her. She has her own pet grooming shop and often puts in twelve-hour days.

combined), and Korea had more education than the average education of native-born Americans. An astonishing 52 percent of all Asian Indians in the United States are college graduates, as are more than one-third of Chinese and Filipino immigrants.

Immigrants are making a particularly valuable contribution to America in the fields of science and medicine. The percentage of first- and second-generation Asian immigrants pursuing graduate degrees in science is several times greater than the Asian percentage of the U.S. population. *BusinessWeek* reported that about 40 percent of the two hundred researchers in the Communications Sciences Wing at AT&T Bell Laboratories were born outside the United States. When I visited the Oak Ridge National Laboratory Energy Research Center a few years ago, the personnel director told me that more than twenty of the staff scientists working at the laboratory were naturalized American citizens originally from China.

Immigrants from the Philippines have made a large contribution to health care in the United States during the past twenty years. An estimated six thousand nurses have been recruited each year to work in this country, and many of them become permanent residents or citizens. Thousands of Philippine doctors practice medicine in America; over four thousand of them through the years have come from one school: the University of Santo Tomas Medical School in Manila.

THESE educated and skilled immigrants would seem to bear no resemblance to the poor and often illiterate "huddled masses" who sailed past the Statue of Liberty in the early years of this century to make America their home. But there is a resemblance, an important one: the shared belief that in America they could have a better life and make more of their abilities than they could anywhere else in the world.

American Values for America

THE GREAT majority of today's immigrants do not have college educations. Most of them, like early-day immigrants, are poor and lacking in special job skills; but also like those who came before, they bring attitudes toward work, family, and education that are valued in America, indeed, that are thought of as truly American values.

Perhaps most important is the immigrant's role in keeping alive America's pioneer spirit. The immigrant as a pioneer is a concept that has impressed many keen observers of American life. Ashley Montague believed that because of immigrants " . . . America still is, as it has never ceased to be, a country of pioneers." As you will recall, President Kennedy also believed that immigrants " . . . kept the pioneer spirit of American life . . . always alive and strong."

Are today's immigrants pioneers? That was a question I had never thought about until I read President Kennedy's book. Pioneers go to new places, unknown places, survive under difficult conditions, make new discoveries, pave the way for others. Immigrants do all those things. They are transported literally overnight from their native land to a strange land where they cannot speak or understand the language, where customs are unfamiliar, transportation bewildering, job search a mystery. They overcome their fear and homesickness, learn the new language, solve the mysteries, and in doing so make immigration a little less difficult for others in their family who may follow.

Most immigrants begin their life in America in big cities where other immigrants from their native country live. That has always been the pattern and still is. But just as 150 years ago immigrant pioneers—Germans, Swedes, Irish—pushed out from East Coast cities to settle and open up the West, so increasing numbers of today's immigrants are leaving their safe-haven cities to live in other parts of the country.

After an examination of 1990 census data, Jeffrey Passel, a demographer for the Urban Institute, reported: "There's a movement of both Asians and Hispanics out of the initial settlement areas into broader distribution across the country."

My personal observations tally with Passel's research. Recently my wife, Martha, and I drove across the country from our home in Williamsburg, Virginia, to Tucson, Arizona. In most places of any size where we stopped I saw at least a few Asian and Hispanic people, sometimes a good many. Unless I had a chance to ask, I did not know whether they were recent immigrants, but most of those I met along the way had come to America during the eighties.

I think our biggest surprise came in discovering that about eight hundred Hmong (pronounced *mong*) refugees from Laos have made their home in Marion, North Carolina, and the surrounding Blue Ridge Mountain country. The Hmong are one of the tragic stories of the Vietnam War, a remote mountain tribe that lives by farming, with little knowledge of the outside world and not even a written language until recent years. Over thirty thousand Hmong men fought for the United States in Southeast Asia, supported by CIA guns and money. After the departure of U.S. troops and the collapse of South Vietnam, the Hmong tribesmen became the focus of Communist wrath and retaliation.

Large numbers of Hmong sought safety in the refugee camps of Thailand, and since 1975 over 100,000 Hmong, in many cases whole families, have come to America. Most were originally settled in large metropolitan areas—Fresno, Minneapolis-St. Paul, Philadelphia—and with few exceptions suffered terrible adjustment problems. After years of struggle, some have won hard-earned places in the cities. But many Hmong have sought more compatible environments in the rural areas of California, Minnesota, Wisconsin, Pennsylvania, and Montana.

The rolling Blue Ridge foothills around Marion must have stirred memories of their Laos home in those who made the journey to North Carolina. The first Hmong arrivals were sponsored by the congregation of the Garden Creek Baptist Church of Marion, who helped with housing and other basic necessities as well as with orientation, job search, and English.

Today in and around this town named for Revolutionary War General Francis Marion, the Swamp Fox, the Hmong are making a new life for themselves. A number of them already own some land, and many are farming. Some have taken training and are working at relatively low-level jobs in area factories and businesses. A few Hmong have risked returning to Laos, but in every case they have come back to Marion. I talked to one returnee and asked him why he had come back.

His answer was simple and clear. "Is better here," he said.

WE MET Cambodians and Afghans in Oklahoma City, and one night we had dinner at a little Vietnamese restaurant in Farmington, New Mexico. America has become fond of the delicate flavors of Vietnamese food, and it can be found in abundance in East and West coast cities. A Vietnamese restaurant in Farmington struck me as trailblazing, but judging from the number of customers who flowed through the restaurant that evening, I guessed that the Vietnamese family was glad they had come to the bustling little city in New Mexico.

WHEN Martha and I are traveling by car in the Southwest, we try to stop in Pecos, Texas, where we have found the Mexican food to be particularly good. Pecos had its moment of fame in Texas history as the town where Judge Roy Bean held court as "the law west of Fort Smith." Today it is a vigorous small south Texas town where Anglos and Mexican Americans seem to make up almost the whole population.

Pecos was just about the last place I would have expected to find a bearded, turbaned Pakistani running a motel. But that is what we found when we checked into a place on the edge of town. He and his family had come from New York two years ago to run the motel, he told me, and he said that south Texas summers reminded him of pre-monsoon weather in Pakistan: hot and dry.

I thought about the Pakistani family setting out from New York, leaving friends, crossing the country, becoming probably the only Pakistani family in Pecos. "You're rather like the pioneers who moved west to settle this country, aren't you?" I said.

"Oh, no, sir," the Pakistani innkeeper replied. "Pioneers came a long time ago. Very brave people."

I didn't argue the point, but I think I could have made a good case that he and his family had the same kind of nerve, hope, and spirit that pioneers in America have always had. And I think the same could be said for the Hmong in Marion and the Vietnamese who opened the restaurant in Farmington.

AMERICANS have traditionally valued work for its own sake and have believed that work is the key to success—a belief known as the "work ethic." Immigrants give us probably the best example we have today of the work ethic. Joe Martha holding three jobs at once in order to get money to bring his family to America is an example. George Aguilar working on a construction job all day and in a restaurant at night is an example. You can look into most immigrant lives and find the same commitment to hard work, the same belief that work is a necessary ingredient of success.

Vietnamese fishermen working out of Gulf Coast ports soon after their arrival in the United States in the late seventies and early eighties were typical of immigrant energy and family effort. They fished long hours into the night. They slept on their boats in order to get an early start. One long-time Gulf fishing-boat owner had this to say about the newcomers: "They've got husbands and wives, brothers, uncles, kids all working together. We don't do things that way. How can we compete with that?"

The presence of the Vietnamese fishermen caused tensions in a few places at first, but they have proved themselves to be good and productive members of their communities. Some Gulf port cities such as Biloxi, Mississippi, have welcomed relatively large numbers of Vietnamese.

Thousands of immigrants have made a success of small businesses: convenience stores, cafes, vegetable and flower stalls, grocery stores, cleaning shops, among many others. Almost without exception the businesses are "mom and pop" operations, pooling family resources, the husband and wife working side by side, day and night, to keep the new venture afloat.

Atanasio and Maritza Navarro could hardly be called the typical immigrant mom and pop, but the energy and effort they have put into making a place for themselves in America is typical of untold thousands of immigrant couples. The Navarros were refugees from Nicaragua, forced to flee when the Sandinistas came to power in that country. Before the national revolution in 1979, the Navarros and their daughter, Rebecca, then five years old, lived a comfortable, prosperous life in the capital city of Managua. Atanasio was a well-established architect, Maritza a government lawyer. It was because Maritza had been a part of the overthrown government that they were in danger.

The Navarros escaped to the neighboring country of Costa Rica and were given refugee status by the American embassy there. Six months later they arrived in Columbia, Missouri, sponsored by Atanasio's brother Manuel, who lived in Columbia. A physician, Manuel had immigrated to the United States in the late 1950s. Having a relative to acquaint them with their new home was a great help to Atanasio and Maritza, but they faced the same problems that almost all immigrants face. They had been able to bring very little money out of Nicaragua; they spoke only a few phrases of English; they were not licensed to practice their professions of architecture and law in the United States.

Atanasio set out to find a job, any kind of job, but for weeks, badly handicapped by his minimal English, he found nothing. Then one day he walked past an eating place with a name he recognized; at least he recognized the words because they were Spanish: TACO TICO. "Taco," of course, is a Spanish word for a tortilla filled with meat. "Tico" is a Nicaraguan name for the people of Costa Rica.

Atanasio rushed into the fast-food place, sure that everyone would speak Spanish. To his dismay he found only Anglos inside, and no one working there spoke Spanish. In his frustration Atanasio just kept repeating "Job! Job! Job!" until the manager of the eatery put him to work. Atanasio's first job in his new homeland was sweeping and mopping floors, washing dishes, and carrying out garbage. But he was happy. He had a job!

Atanasio began to learn English, picked up other jobs, and sometimes was working ninety hours a week. Maritza also tried to find work but with no success. They were living in a trailer at that time, and she spent her days and nights looking after Rebecca. Her life was totally different from what it had been in Managua where she had worked as a lawyer, had a home, and a maid to look after Rebecca during the day.

"I spent a lot of my time in the trailer crying," Maritza will tell you now.

After several months Atanasio met Pon Chinn, a long-established architect in Columbia. Chinn offered Atanasio a job as draftsman, and he took it, happy to be able to use some part of his architect background again. The job did not last long, however, because Chinn's son-in-law returned to take a place in the firm as draftsman, and there was no longer a position for Atanasio. But in a most unlikely combination of architecture and the food business, Pon Chinn owned a Dunkin' Donuts shop, and he offered to let Atanasio and Maritza manage it.

"But we don't know anything about doughnuts!" Atanasio told Chinn.

Chinn assured him that they would learn, so they took over the shop and ran it for a year. Then Chinn decided to open a Chinese fast-food restaurant and asked the Navarros to run it.

"But we don't know anything about Chinese food!" Atanasio protested.

"You told me that about doughnuts," Chinn reminded him, "but you learned."

Pon Chinn had come to America with his immigrant parents when he was nine years old and had worked his way through architectural school. Drawing on a lifetime of experience, he said to Atanasio, "There is unlimited opportunity in the United States. You can do anything you want if you work hard. The American people will give you the chance if you prove yourself."

Atanasio and Maritza did learn about Chinese food from the cook at the Wok In, which is what Pon Chinn called his restaurant. And they learned about managing a fast-food restaurant. They learned so well that after another year Atanasio wanted to start his own fast-food restaurant, and since Chinese food was what they had learned to cook, the easy decision was that the new venture should be a Chinese fast-food restaurant.

"Life is such a surprise," Maritza says. "Before, in Nicaragua, I never liked to cook."

Atanasio borrowed enough money from his brother to start the restaurant, and he and Maritza found an empty two-story building in downtown Jefferson City, about thirty miles distant from Columbia. They didn't want their restaurant to compete with the Wok In of Pon Chinn.

Jefferson City is the capital of Missouri, and the Navarros had a good location for their restaurant, only a few blocks from the capitol itself. Their building needed extensive remodeling to make it into a restaurant, and the Navarros decided to make the upper floor into their home. For the first time in several years Atanasio was able to use his experience and talents as an architect, and he plunged happily into the task of planning and building their new business and their new home in America. At night the Navarros worked on the menu for their restaurant, which they decided to call The American Wok. The menu when

Atanasio and Maritza Navarro with their daughter, Rebecca. Rebecca, now eighteen, is a senior at Helias High School in Jefferson City. She is a member of the National Honor Society and the U.S. Naval Sea Cadet Corps. Rebecca intends to become a lawyer, following in her mother's footsteps.

completed offered thirty-five choices, among them such Chinese restaurant favorites as Szechuan chicken, twice-cooked pork, and beef lo mein.

The American Wok opened its doors on September 7, 1983. The restaurant, now past its tenth anniversary, has become a solid part of the Jefferson City downtown business community. The loan which enabled the Navarros to start the restaurant has been repaid. A highlight came in 1990 when Atanasio and Maritza received a Mid-Missouri Minority Business Award. The letter from Governor John Ashcroft announcing the award praised the Navarros' "extraordinary initiative" and the quality of their restaurant. In his letter, the governor remarked that he had personally enjoyed eating at The American Wok.

In the beginning The American Wok was a classic example of the "mom and pop" immigrant operation with either Atanasio or Maritza or both on duty at all times. They are still very much on the job but now have a small staff to help. Atanasio has given a good deal of thought to opening a second American Wok in another part of Jefferson City, but neither of the Navarros has abandoned the idea that they might someday practice their original professions as architect and lawyer in Missouri. Maritza is now taking courses toward a master's degree at a local university, and Atanasio is considering enrolling in drafting school.

But he is also thinking about going to computer school, which Maritza has done already. "Today," says Atanasio, "everybody should know computers."

Whatever they decide for the future, the Navarros have proved the soundness of Pon Chinn's words about what hard work can accomplish in America.

THE United States has always put the strong, supportive family at the top of the list of what is important to us as a nation, as the main source of our strength as a country. In the latter part of the twentieth century, the apparent deterioration of family relationships has become a major concern that preoccupies church, government, and millions of individual Americans.

If we need a clear example of family solidarity and its importance, we need look no further than today's immigrants. The supportive, close-knit family has marked immigrant life in America from the beginning and has not changed even to the present time. Writing about Asian Americans, both recent immigrants and those who have been here for a long time, historian David Bell says that family stability "contributes to success in at least three ways. First, it provides a secure environment for children. Second, it pushes those children to do better than their parents. And finally, it is a significant financial advantage." A Population Reference Bureau study cites census data to show that " . . . It is common within Asian-American families to pool resources for housing, schooling, and other needs, particularly in the first years in the U.S."

Probably most of us know or have met immigrants who are part of a closely integrated large family. As Jennifer and I have worked together on books for the last several years, we have watched an extended family from Afghanistan in the condominium complex where she lives. The first to arrive were a husband and wife and two children, refugees from the political fury in their country. They lived in a rented apartment and found work. As they became established, they sponsored other family members who were languishing in the refugee camps of Pakistan, which borders Afghanistan.

Slowly the family grew, parents, brothers, sisters, small children joining those who had already come. The Afghans rented other apartments; the young men helped each other find jobs; the children went to school. The big family divided their labors. Some women took care of the small children to free working time for others. Some washed clothes for the extended family. They pooled their money and bought two of the apartments they had been renting.

In the fall of 1991 one of the young Afghan men, the first in his family, graduated from high school and enrolled in college.

Dr. Mohammad Akhter, the Pakistani immigrant who is commissioner of health for the District of Columbia, also talked to me about family. He and his wife have brought her parents and his parents to live with them. Dr. Akhter's mother is seventy-eight, his father eighty. "Every morning as I leave for work, I get a kiss from my mother on one cheek and from my mother-in-law on the other, and they both wish me a safe and happy day," Dr. Akhter said. "For me, there is no sweeter pleasure in life."

Americans have traditionally wanted the best education possible for their children. So have immigrants. In fact, the deciding factor in parents' decision to immigrate often has been the desire to give their children a chance for the best possible education. We have already seen how America is benefiting from the extraordinary drive for higher education of Asian Americans.

An Asian-American university professor seemed to sum up how millions of immigrants feel about education when he said, "Except for freedom, education is America's greatest treasure, and everyone can share in it. Why shouldn't we?"

Do Immigrants Take Jobs Away from Other Americans?

THE MOST emotional question regarding immigrants is not whether they bring strange customs, languages, and religions to America, not whether they are somehow changing the American way of life. The concern of the great majority of Americans who have negative feelings about immigrants is a very practical one: do they take jobs away from other Americans?

That question, that fear, has created controversy about immigration for at least 150 years. The Chicago riots of the 1850s against Irish immigrants stemmed from a fear that they might increase competition for jobs. Labor unions have traditionally been wary of immigration for the same reasons and for the fear that increased competition might push down wages. However, some industries and businesses that need low-income workers—agriculture, motels and hotels, restaurants, fast-food places—insist that they would find meeting their staff needs almost impossible without immigrants.

Many well-qualified researchers and research organizations have agreed that job displacement by immigrants is not a serious problem for the nation as a whole, particularly in reasonably good economic times. Julian L. Simon reviews a number of job displacement research studies in *The Economic Consequences of Immigration* and concludes that the studies " . . . suggest that general immigration causes little or no unemployment at large. . . ." And Simon continues that immigrants " . . . open new businesses that employ natives as well as other immigrants and themselves. And they do so in important numbers—small businesses are now the most important source of new jobs."

A study by the Urban Institute concludes that " . . . the influx of Mexicans to Los Angeles and southern California during the 1970s did not increase the aggregate level of unemployment among non-Hispanic California residents, including blacks." According to a 1985 study by the Rand Corporation: "Our evidence suggests that Mexican immigration has provided a boost to California's economy, especially in the Los Angeles area, by enabling many low-wage industries to continue to expand at a time when their counterparts were contracting in the face of foreign competition." In other words, without a good supply of people willing to work for low wages, some industries would have gone out of business or moved to Mexico.

Many Americans will not take boring, dead-end jobs that pay the minimum wage of $4.25 an hour. Newly arrived immigrants take such jobs willingly and hope in time to move up the ladder. The owner of a cleaning service in Reston, Virginia, reported that she tried to hire teenagers for hourly wages ranging from $4.25 to $4.75 an hour but that they would quit after working only a short time. When she turned to hiring Hispanic immigrants, her staffing problems disappeared. They stayed on the job.

Leon Bouvier and Robert W. Gardner in "Immigration to the U.S.: The Unfinished Story" write: "To sum up the questions on immigrants' impact on the U.S. economy, there appears to be agreement, albeit tentative, that legal immigration, particularly if it is funneled into the white-collar sector (as with much immigration from Asia), serves to produce more jobs for the overall economy."

Probably, all of these studies are accurate. But in difficult economic times, people out of a job and looking for work must wonder about the million new immigrants who arrive each year. Convincing them that these newcomers don't increase competition in the job market would not be easy.

Other Questions About Immigrants

THE WORK, energy and vigor that immigrants bring to their new homeland is generally acknowledged, but do they receive more in social services—education, public housing, unemployment compensation, health care, and other welfare benefits—than they pay in taxes? There is no clear answer, just as there is none to the question about whether immigrants take jobs from other Americans.

The Council of Economic Advisers, a group of distinguished American economists who advise the executive branch of the federal government, believes that immigrants more than pay their way. In a detailed report on immigration the council concluded that " . . . immigrants provide a net fiscal benefit to the nation, often paying more in taxes than they use in public services." Maryland University professor Julian Simon, in his study of the economics of immigration, also concludes that " . . . immigrants contribute more to the public coffers than they take from them."

Researchers who have analyzed immigrants' use of unemployment insurance point out that some immigrants do not apply for such insurance or for welfare assistance for fear of harming their chances of becoming citizens or because they do not understand that they may be eligible. Instead, during times of unemployment, they seek support from other family members. A recent Population Reference Bureau study found that " . . . Data from the 1980 census indicate that Asian Americans are very little burden on state and federal public assistance resources." An exception to this generalization, the study noted, was the considerable government support given to post-Vietnam Southeast Asian refugees until they became well established.

The above generalizations are made on the basis of national averages. When certain types of immigrants and certain specific locations are studied, the findings can be quite different. For example, an Immigration and Naturalization Services study in 1983 calculated that each 1 million *illegal* immigrants receives $1.26 billion more in education, health, and other social services than they pay in taxes. Illegal immigrants cannot apply for welfare benefits because they do not have the proper documents. But they often receive health care—particularly of an emergency nature—since hospitals and health clinics rarely check immigrant status before providing services. And the Supreme Court has ruled that children of illegal immigrants must be admitted to elementary and high schools. (The children are not in the United States of their own freewill and should not be deprived of education because their parents are illegal aliens.)

An Urban Institute study found that the city of Los Angeles incurs a net loss of $2,245 per *recent* immigrant family. It can be argued that when legal immigrant families become established their contributions to the tax base increase, and other studies have found this to be true.

A MUCH more emotional question is whether the large-scale presence of immigrants in some cities is a detriment to the success of African Americans who may have lived in those cities for a long time. Without doubt the newcomers increase competition for jobs and put a strain on limited city social services. Recent studies at Chicago University indicate that employers, even in low-wage industries, prefer to hire immigrants rather than African Americans.

Except for the Chicago University studies, I know of no reliable research on the subject of whether some immigrant success comes at the expense of African Americans. Nevertheless, many African Americans firmly believe that it does. This belief has led to the boycotting of immigrant businesses in Washington, D.C., to the picketing of Korean greengrocers in New York City, to the burning of Asian-American stores during the Los Angeles riots. Immigrants protest that they are minorities, too, and that minorities should support one another.

It is true that in many cities immigrants have found successful places for themselves in largely black areas. But as long as massive urban poverty and a large urban underclass exist, tensions will exist between immigrants and African Americans in some cities.

STILL another question about immigrants is that of language. Some Americans feel that English as the unifying language of our country is threatened by recent trends in immigration. A hundred years ago, they say, European immigrants wanted to learn English as fast as possible. Today there are large areas of U.S. cities where Spanish or Vietnamese is heard more often than English. The new immigrants from Latin America and Asia, say those who worry about the language purity of the United States, aren't interested in learning English. An organization called U.S. English is dedicated to having English declared the "official"

Volunteer teacher Cheryl Pendell conducting an English-language class at Columbia Baptist Church in Falls Church, Virginia. Hundreds of churches, schools, and other organizations offer free English instruction for adult immigrants. Although Spanish is widely spoken in some parts of the United States, a reasonable command of English is considered in almost all parts of the country as essential to economic advancement for Hispanics, Asians, and all other immigrant groups.

language of the United States. By 1990 seventeen states had passed laws designating English as the official language of their state.

Is English really an endangered language? Nonsense, say most language experts who study the matter. On the contrary, English continues to gain prominence as the major world language. Without question it is the language of business around the world. Long ago English replaced French as the language of diplomacy. English is a part of the school curriculum in most countries of Europe, Africa, and Asia, and is widely taught in Latin America. In the past five years the Peace Corps has started programs in many countries of former Communist Europe. What these countries request more than anything else is volunteers to teach English.

It is true that in a few places in the United States, mostly in cities, Spanish, Vietnamese, and Korean are widely spoken, and that may continue; but the ability to speak English is still essential to economic success almost everywhere in the country, and immigrants who want to succeed will learn English. A knowledge of English remains a requirement for citizenship, and more immigrants are applying for citizenship every year than can be tested. The magazine *Hispanic* (for and about Hispanics but published in English) complains that there are long waiting lists for English classes in most schools and other places where English training is offered.

I have never talked to a language expert who did not believe that English will continue to be the dominant language of the United States. At the same time most have expressed the thought that a greater awareness of and appreciation of other languages—particularly Spanish—is a good thing for Americans, both culturally and economically, in today's diverse and interdependent global society.

A Note on Immigrant Failures

NOT ALL immigrants to America succeed at even a minimum level. As we have already seen, 2 million or more illegal immigrants—most of them poor and uneducated—live in the United States. They are prohibited by federal law from holding jobs; even those who manage to find work hardly ever earn a living wage. Most of them are a burden to society or to relatives they may live with.

Thousands of legal immigrants, also poor and uneducated, have arrived in the United States in recent years. In most cases they are refugees from Southeast Asia and Central America whose lives were disrupted, often for years, by war and political turmoil. Many have had no schooling. Adult refugees in this category have a hard time learning enough English and making other adjustments to qualify for even the lowest levels of service jobs. According to a San Diego State University study of six hundred refugees in that city, three-quarters of them were living below the official government poverty line and about 60 percent were on welfare. The study reports that the refugees "are preponderantly marginal, poor families living in crowded conditions in low-rent districts of San Diego, typically sharing their apartments with extended family members and friends." Many other large U.S. cities have groups of "marginal" legal immigrants such as the ones in San Diego.

The children of these immigrants have an equally difficult time. A 1992 *Washington Post* article reports, "Some of the teenage immigrants . . . have missed so much school that catching up and getting their diplomas is a herculean task, teachers said. The older they are when they arrive, the less time they have to catch up, and some students never do."

The article quotes the director of the English for Speakers of Other Languages program at a suburban Maryland high school as saying, "For every success story, there are two failures." He was speaking of immigrant students who arrive with little or no formal education.

The failures of the severely disadvantaged newcomers are a sad aspect of our national immigration picture, but they do not negate the fact that most of today's legal immigrants in time find a measure of success in the United States. Often the success is minimal but usually an improvement on what they would have achieved in their native land. For many immigrants, their eventual success is substantial, equaling that of native-born Americans with comparable education or skills. And, also in percentages comparable to those of the native born, a smaller number of immigrants reach the top professionally and economically. Immigrants from all of these levels of success are continuing to make the kinds of civic and cultural contributions that immigrants have always made to America. They are the immigrants I have chosen to write about in this book.

4

Becoming an American

> . . . *I will support and defend the Constitution and laws of the United States of America against all enemies, foreign and domestic* . . .
>
> From the Oath of Allegiance taken
> by all naturalized citizens

Chinese New Year parade, Washington, D.C.

To Be a Citizen

BECOMING a United States citizen through the process of naturalization is not easy. The immigrant must live in the United States for at least five years as a legal resident before he or she can apply for citizenship. The applicant must furnish full biographic information, fill out forms about payment of taxes and police records, and submit photographs and fingerprint charts.

Finally, persons applying for naturalization must have a knowledge and understanding of the history, principles, and form of government of the United States. They are also examined on their ability to read, write, and speak English. Persons more than fifty years of age who have been lawful permanent residents of the United States for twenty years or more are exempt from the English language requirements of the law. They may take the examination in the language they customarily speak.

Permanent resident immigrants do not have to become citizens of the United States. In fact, almost half of all foreign-born residents do not. There are many reasons why immigrants may spend much of their lives in America and never take the step to citizenship. Their children born in the United States are automatically citizens, and for some immigrants that is enough. For some the English language hurdle is too great; that is especially the case for older immigrants who have come to live with their adult immigrant children. Some find renouncing the citizenship of their native homeland too painful. For others the status of citizen does not seem especially important.

Permanent legal residents have almost all rights and responsibilities that native-born and naturalized citizens have. They can own property, start businesses, send their children to school, live anywhere in the country they desire. They are subject to all laws and pay local, state, and federal taxes just as citizens do.

Some government, law enforcement, and aerospace jobs are restricted to citizens. Some federal aid and scholarships are for citizens only. U.S. citizens can petition to get relatives (parents, brothers, sisters) into the United States, while permanent resident noncitizens can petition only for entry of spouse and children. Leaving and reentering the United States is easier for citizens than for noncitizens.

The above citizen's rights and privileges can be important in individual cases. But there is a much more important difference—a fundamental difference—between citizens and noncitizens. Only citizens of the United States can vote in governmental elections and only citizens can hold federal and most other public offices. Probably most immigrants who become citizens do not do so just to gain the right to vote and to hold public office. But those rights are fundamental to the very concept of representative democracy on which our nation was founded, and without them an immigrant can never be a full partner in his adopted land.

DR. JAY W. KHIM is a naturalized citizen of the United States, and his years in America add up to a storybook tale of immigrant success. From the beginning he was not a typical or average immigrant. The

Dr. Jay H. Khim.

son of a successful apple grower and exporter in Korea, he received a bachelor's and master's degree in economics from Kyungpook National University in Korea. He served as a second lieutenant in the Korean Army after graduating from officers' school at the top of his class.

In the early 1960s, Khim received a U.S. government Fulbright Scholarship and attended the University of Maryland to pursue a Ph.D. degree in economics. His father had died when Khim was fourteen, and the modest family fortune was used to support the family. By the time he finished his studies at Maryland, family funds were exhausted. Khim decided to stay in America and with his excellent education had no trouble becoming a permanent resident.

From the beginning Jay Khim found America fertile ground for his talents. He spent several years at the Brookings Institute in Washington, D.C. Brookings is one of America's top "think tanks," and Khim carried out research in international technology transfer and economic development. After Brookings he became a senior economist at the National Alliance of Businessmen and then a senior associate at the Planning Research Corporation.

In 1973 Dr. Khim decided to form his own research and planning company. The result was JWK International Corporation, which in twenty years has grown from an initial five employees to three hundred staff members with highly professional backgrounds. Khim's company has completed hundreds of government research and technical assistance contracts. The company has helped the U.S. Department of Transportation with urban mass transportation planning, the agriculture department with marketing programs, the health and human services department with health care financing. JWK has helped the Department of Defense with planning for weapons systems acquisitions, logistics, and international security.

"We are in the knowledge business," Dr. Khim told me.

The knowledge business has made Jay Khim a wealthy man, and for many people building a hugely successful company would have been enough. But it wasn't enough for Khim. He wanted to participate fully in the life of his adopted country, including the political life, and he knew he could not do that without becoming a citizen. The decision was not an easy one to make. He had had a good life in Korea; his family and close friends were there; he had served in the army of his country. Khim discussed the question of citizenship with his American friends. He even talked with Senator William Fulbright, then chairman

Jay Khim on the campaign trail.

of the Senate Foreign Relations Committee, whom he had met through the scholarship program.

"I agonized over the decision," Dr. Khim said. "To be a citizen I knew I would have to take an oath even to bear arms against my former homeland if necessary."

But at the end of his mental debate, Khim knew that he was already an American in thought and feeling, and so he became a citizen. He lost no time in becoming an active participant in the civic life of his new homeland, and he has remained active through the years. A registered Republican, he took part in party activities in the Washington area. He has been on the board of directors of the Fairfax, Virginia, Chamber of Commerce, and was co-chairman of the League of Korean Americans. He has served on the board of directors of the Fairfax Hospital System and on the advisory board of the Immigration and Naturalization Service.

Khim had never previously given serious thought to running for public office, but in 1992 he exercised that citizen's important right when he ran for Congress in the Virginia Eleventh Congressional District. An economist and businessman, he based his campaign primarily on the need to reduce the country's staggering national debt, balance the budget, and create jobs by revitalizing America's industrial strength. Khim did not win, but he made a good showing for the hotly contested congressional seat.

I talked with Dr. Khim in his JWK office soon after the election. He talked about politics and also about the contributions that Korean Americans and other Asian Americans make to the country. He spoke of family unity, the stable home and strong support that most Asian-American parents give their children, the way they help their children achieve excellence in education. On a table beside his desk was a photograph of Khim and his wife with their son and daughter. His son, he told me, was a physician, his daughter a lawyer.

"My mother lives with us," Khim said. "She is eighty-four. You know, most Asians can't imagine sending their parents to a nursing home. Their place is in the home."

I asked Dr. Khim if he intended to run for Congress again.

"It is much too early to say," he answered. "We will see what happens and what the conditions are in two years. I don't know. But this is America, and the door is always open."

ATANASIO and Maritza, the Nicaraguan refugees who opened a successful Chinese fast-food restaurant in Jefferson City, Missouri, have another accomplishment that they are vastly more proud of. As quickly as they could after their required five years of residence, they became citizens of the United States. On July 3, 1986, they took the Oath of Allegiance, and they were especially pleased that the ceremony was held at the Truman Library in Independence.

When they returned to Jefferson City, Atanasio had a big Statue of

The Navarros celebrate their new citizenship.

Liberty spray-painted on the plate-glass window of The American Wok together with the words WE ARE PROUD TO BE AMERICANS. Many of their friends and customers helped celebrate the big event by showering them with telegrams, phone calls, flowers, cakes, and other gifts.

The Civic Life

AMERICANS—immigrants and native born—can enter into the civic life of our country in many ways besides voting and holding public office. We can let our elected officials know how we feel about public issues. The Navarros wrote a letter to President Reagan in support of his Nicaragua policy and were astonished to receive a personal reply from the president. We can take part in public forums on matters that are important to us. The day before she became a citizen, Maritza Navarro spoke to the twenty-fifth annual Missouri Freedom Forum. She drew on the experiences that had made her a refugee for her topic, "Freedom: Do We Take It for Granted?"

According to public opinion surveys, there is a strong feeling among Americans that a good citizen is one who takes part in community affairs. Immigrants are often slow to participate in the public life of the places where they live for several reasons: they may lack or feel that they lack English skills; they are uncertain about whether they will be welcome; they are totally occupied with work and adjustment to their new life; they simply do not know how they can participate.

Many ethnic minorities in America have addressed the problem of participation by forming associations and organizations that help the adjustment of new immigrants and encourage all members of the ethnic group to take part in community activities. Any big-city telephone directory will reveal a long list of such organizations: the Korean-American Chamber of Commerce, the Ethiopian Community Development Council, the Vietnamese Mutual Assistance Association, and dozens more. In some places voter registration of immigrant citizens is an important activity. The Southwest Voter Registration Education Project in Texas and California has dramatically increased the number of Hispanic voters in those states. Many are first-generation immigrants.

Schools in many large cities have a great need for ethnic minority participation in parent-teacher and other school activities. The same problems of language, uncertainty, and lack of time hold back many immigrant parents from taking part in school activities, but that is changing. The National Association of Latino Elected and Appointed Officials recently reported that across the nation over 4,000 Hispanics now hold public office. Of that number nearly 1,600 have been elected or appointed to school boards, and a good many are immigrants.

In St. Paul, Minnesota, in 1991 Choua Lee, a Hmong who came

to America from Laos as a refugee when she was a child, waged a vigorous campaign and won a seat on the city school board. Ms. Lee is twenty-three and a graduate of Mankato University in Minnesota. She is the first Hmong to be elected to public office in the United States.

"I'm Hmong, and that's my perspective; it's how I grew up," she said after her victory. "But we live in St. Paul, and St. Paul is a great, diverse city. There are a lot of groups that need to learn about each other. I plan to help."

IMMIGRANT participation in the civic life of a community can take many forms, but the involvement of Jean-Keith Fagon in his community is one of the most unusual examples. Jean-Keith was born in the tiny village of Grantham, located deep in the hills of Clarendon Parish in Jamaica. He grew up there and graduated with top honors in science from Clarendon College. Jean-Keith was offered a scholarship for graduate study in England, but he had an older brother in Washington, D.C., and he had long dreamed of following his brother and living in America's capital city. That is what he did, arriving in the late sixties and enrolling in Washington's Federal City College.

Jean-Keith received a scholarship from the English Department of Johns Hopkins University in nearby Baltimore and graduated from that highly regarded school with a master's degree in creative writing. He stayed in Washington, but instead of pursuing a writing career, he developed the idea of creating a community newspaper for Washington's Capitol Hill.

The very concept of Capitol Hill as a community might seem strange to many people. The Capitol Hill area is dominated by the great buildings of our national government: the majestic Capitol building itself, the Library of Congress, the Cannon Building, the Longworth Building, and other vast Senate and House of Representative office buildings. The Supreme Court is there. Millions of tourists pour onto "the Hill" every year to see and visit these landmarks.

Yet Capitol Hill is an urban community where over fifty thousand

Jean-Keith Fagon.

people live, people of all races, religions, and ethnic groups. Scores of businesses are located there, most of them small. Doctors, lawyers, architects, and other professionals have offices there. Schools and churches are a part of Capitol Hill.

Jean-Keith brought out the first issue of *The Hill Rag* in 1976, and it was little more than an advertising flier for the few Capitol Hill merchants willing to take a chance on the new publication. Jean-Keith had no money, but he had a vision of which he never let go. Today, over fifteen years later, *The Hill Rag* is a twice-monthly newspaper, each issue with a beautiful full-color cover often featuring a Capitol

Hill scene. The paper regularly carries stories about people who live on the Hill. Other stories deal with subjects which concern Hill residents: the quality of schools, racial and ethnic understanding, the condition of streets and parks, housing, business development, crime. There is no doubt that *The Hill Rag* has become the voice of the Capitol Hill community and that it has helped give this very special area a greater sense of community.

Jean-Keith furthered that sense of community when, several years ago, he took the lead in starting the Capitol Hill Association of Merchants and Professionals (CHAMPS). The association in turn started the CHAMPS Foundation, which makes grants to schools and civic organizations on Capitol Hill. Typical grants have been for funds to start a softball league, special social worker activities, a tutoring program, a summer program in the arts, and a high school computer lab. Over two hundred businesses, professionals, and neighborhood residents have contributed to the CHAMPS Foundation since it was started.

Several years ago Jean-Keith decided that *The Hill Rag* should have a more dignified name to go with its hard-earned prominence on Capitol Hill. He announced a contest to find the new name and was shocked at the outcry of protest. The Capitol Hill merchants and especially the neighborhood readers wouldn't hear of a name change. They had lived with the "Rag" for a long time. It was their newspaper, and they liked the name just the way it was. Jean-Keith quietly cancelled the contest.

The Hill Rag has consumed a large part of his life, and Jean-Keith wants to make it the best community newspaper in the country. When he talks about how he started the paper with only an idea and no money, he echoes the words and thoughts of many immigrants.

"This never could have happened in Jamaica," he will tell you. "There is no way a person can start there with nothing but an idea and build it into what I have here. I know it doesn't always happen, but I think the United States is the best place in the world for making dreams come true."

DREAMS don't always come true. They didn't for Harry Opoku when he came to America. He was born in the African country of Ghana, grew up there, went to high school and college there. He was a gifted soccer player, a star defender on both his high school and college teams. He was drafted by a professional soccer team and quit college to play the sport internationally for three years. When a professional soccer team, the Diplomats, was formed in Washington, D.C., in the seventies, Harry came to Washington to try out. He didn't make the team, but, as it turned out, that didn't make much difference. Washington wasn't ready for professional soccer, and the team folded after a few seasons.

Harry liked living in the United States and was able to get permanent resident status. He went into the import-export business but didn't have the capital to make it a success. He held various jobs after that and has worked for an industrial cleaning company in northern Virginia for almost ten years now. He married an immigrant from Ghana, and they have two children, a daughter and son.

Harry thought that soccer was no longer a part of his life, but he was wrong. His son, who is eleven, has inherited or acquired some of his father's soccer ability and plays forward on a youth club team. Watching practice one day, Harry saw that the coaches could use some technical assistance. He asked if he could help and was enthusiastically welcomed. He soon discovered that there are several teams of different ages and that they play other teams in the area and take part once a year in an international competition. When Harry's soccer experience and coaching ability became known, other local teams asked for his help. To the extent of his free time, he was happy to give it and to travel with the teams when they play out of town. Occasionally someone commends Harry for the valuable community service he is rendering. Harry is always surprised by the praise. He is having fun.

MY Filipino-American friend, Horatio Lotuaco, is a naturalized citizen and proud of his citizenship. But Horatio once said to me, "It is not

Harry Opoku.

simply a piece of paper that makes you an American. Rather, it is a feeling of belonging and a deep conviction that you are one. If you have that feeling and that conviction, you *are* an American."

I agree with Horatio. I also believe that immigrants develop that "feeling," that "deep conviction" by knowing the essentials of American history, by respecting our traditions, and by taking part, in the best ways they can, in the civic life of their communities and of the country.

5

One Nation Indivisible?

These States are the amplest poem.
Here is not merely a nation but a teeming Nation of
   nations.

Walt Whitman

A dragon greets the Year of the Monkey in a Washington, D.C., Chinatown parade. Chinese New Year parades, held in many U.S. cities, are among the oldest ethnic celebrations in America.

IN 1873 Congress passed a law specifying that every U.S. coin must bear the inscription *E pluribus unum*, a Latin phrase meaning "Out of many, one." The law has never been changed, and you will see the phrase on every coin minted today: penny, nickel, dime, quarter, and half dollar.

Debate prior to the law's passage makes clear that the motto was intended to emphasize the unity of the states of the Union: out of many *states*, one *nation*. Only eight years had passed since the end of the Civil War, and national unity was not a matter of academic theory but a burning political issue. Congress wanted to impress on the citizenry that we were one nation of states that could not be divided from each other. That is what we have become insofar as our political subdivisions are concerned: one nation indivisible. No American today seriously considers any other possibility.

Did the 1873 Congress also intend *E pluribus unum* to apply to the people of the nation: out of many different kinds of people, one people? No evidence exists in the Congressional Record that the law-

115

makers had any such thought, but the question of how our nation's many ethnic, racial, and religious groups relate to each other preoccupies us today with the same intensity that the unity of the nation's states concerned Americans over a hundred years ago. What does *E pluribus unum* mean when we are a nation made up of so many cultures and races?

Preoccupation with this question is by no means new. Benjamin Franklin worried about how German immigrants could be made to be like Englishmen. Abraham Lincoln both spoke and wrote about racism and religious and ethnic hatred and called correcting those evils "one of the highest functions of civilization." In 1908 Israel Zangwill, a Jewish immigrant, wrote a play entitled *The Melting Pot*, which was about America as a land where (to quote one of the characters) "all the races of Europe are melting and reforming." The assimilation—or lack of assimilation—of immigrant ethnic groups into the mainstream culture of America had been the subject of many writers before Zangwill, but his phrase, "the melting pot," caught the public's fancy as an easy explanation of the process of assimilation. "Melting pot" has become a standard part of our language and has even made its way into our dictionaries.

Many people today say that the idea of America as a melting pot is a myth or even false. As with most catchy phrases, "melting pot" is only partly accurate as a description of our country. The United States is not a melting pot in which immigrants and their descendants have mixed together to produce Americans who all look alike, think alike, talk alike, worship alike, dress alike, eat alike. The melting pot concept is accurate, however, in the sense that over time the people who live permanently in the United States—those born here as well as immigrants—are brought together in many ways. They are under the same government and subject to the same laws. They share ideas about freedom and responsibility. The Constitution and its Bill of Rights apply to them in the same way. They work together. They watch the same television programs, read the same newspapers, enjoy the same sports.

Most speak English, although millions have learned it as a second language.

At the same time most ethnic groups in America—African Americans, Native Americans, Chinese Americans, Mexican Americans, Italian Americans, and many, many others—have retained some of their customs and traditions. The members enjoy their group's festivals, dances, foods. They retain a number of its values. Many have close relatives in the country they or their parents or grandparents came from, and they continue to care about what happens to that country. Many still speak the language of their ancestral country or group, and in some cases their children speak it. Most large American cities have sections where one ethnic group or another lives close together and does business together. Scores of American Indian tribes have made strong efforts to retain their language and their special relationship with the physical and spiritual world.

With this kind of ethnic group separation, with this kind of clinging to the traditions of ancestral cultures, how can it be said that we are "one nation indivisible"? How can we pretend that the motto *E pluribus unum* has any meaning except as a description of the states of the Union?

Judge Cruz Reynoso was the first Mexican American to serve on the California Supreme Court; he also served on the congressional Select Commission on Immigration and Refugee Policy. He explains our national unity in this way: "Americans are not now, and never have been *one* people linguistically or ethnically. America is a political union—not a cultural, linguistic, religious, or racial union. It is acceptance of our Constitutional ideals of democracy, equality, and freedom which acts as a unifier for us as Americans."

Many people would argue that the English language and British heritage in general have been powerful unifiers of our country, but it is true that other languages and cultures have been a part of America since colonial days. These different languages and cultures have found common ground in the ideals of democracy as expressed in the Constitution.

Holding the dragons' heads in the Chinese New Year parade.

Other images have been suggested as a more accurate alternative to "melting pot" to describe America's cultural unity. Some writers have used the analogy of a tapestry: many threads of different colors are woven together to produce a coherent pattern. Lawrence H. Fuchs, Professor of American Civilization and Politics at Brandeis University, has used the image of a kaleidoscope. A quilt or tapestry forms patterns which do not change. A kaleidoscope also forms patterns out of dissimilar shapes and colors, but the patterns change constantly, just as America's ethnic cultures change over time.

The following passage from Professor Fuchs' book, *The American Kaleidoscope: Race, Ethnicity, and the Civic Culture,* offers a fine explanation of how and why America can flourish as a multicultural society:

"The civic culture was based essentially . . . on three ideas widely held by the founders of the republic, the ideas that constituted what they called republicanism: first, that ordinary men and women can be trusted to govern themselves through their elected representatives, who are accountable to the people; second, that all who live in the political community . . . are eligible to participate in public life as equals; and third, that individuals who comport themselves as good citizens of the civic culture are free to differ from each other in religion and in other aspects of their private lives.

"That third idea was the basis for a kind of voluntary pluralism in which immigrant settlers from Europe and their progeny were free to maintain affection for and loyalty to their ancestral religions and cultures while at the same time claiming an American identity by embracing the founding myths and participating in the political life of the republic."

MANY parts of the world today are being torn apart by savage ethnic, racial, and religious strife. Yugoslavia is a horrifying example; equally tragic examples can be found in Africa and Asia. The recent falling apart of the Soviet Union did not stem primarily from ethnic antagonisms, but the breakup, when it came, was along ethnic, racial, and religious lines.

Some Americans, seeing the dismal world picture, view our own country's growing cultural diversity with alarm. What they forget is that in almost all cases the countries or empires that are suffering these cultural conflicts were originally formed by military conquest or were put together by international political decisions at the end of World War I and World War II. To the contrary, the population of the United States has grown primarily from immigrants who wanted to come to this country, and their descendents. In many cases immigrants have come and continue to come to escape ethnic strife that has engulfed their former homelands.

Pride in ethnic roots and cultures was kindled by the civil and human rights struggles of the 1960s. That pride burns even more brightly today. Surely this is a good thing because it helps us to define America in a way that includes everyone. Now, as never before in our country, we are making an effort to understand and *appreciate* our cultural differences. The end result of this effort can hardly be anything but good for our country. Some people fear that emphasizing our diversity will drive wedges between us, but our national unity will be damaged only if ethnic groups isolate themselves and try to assert a cultural or moral superiority.

The growing cultural and racial diversity of America does make our pursuit of shared values and national goals of crucial importance. One common goal is the fuller understanding and appreciation of our diversity. Another is the fuller participation of all ethnic and minority groups in the civic culture of the country. The value that Americans of all ethnic groups and races put on family, educational attainment, honest work, and allegiance to our constitutional ideals of civil rights and liberties can help to make us a more unified people.

Can we make *E pluribus unum* mean "out of many cultures and races a people united"? Time alone will tell, but we already know this: only we the people can make it happen.

6

The Next Chapter:
Immigration in the
Nineties and Beyond

" . . . the American nationality is still forming: its processes are mysterious, and the final form, if there is ever to be a final form, is as yet unknown."

Nathan Glazer and Daniel P. Moynihan
in *Beyond the Melting Pot*

The Lincoln Memorial has special meaning for Americans of all ethnic backgrounds.

AS America stands on the threshold of the twenty-first century, immigration is as much a part of our national life as it has ever been. We are still a nation of immigrants in the sense that today's newcomers—like all immigrants before them—are playing a part in defining what it means to be an American and in adding vitality to our country and variety to our culture.

The present pattern of large-scale Asian and Latin American immigration is almost certain to continue, bringing increasing cultural diversity to the United States. Our immigration picture will always change, however, in response to world events. The collapse of Communism and the breakup of the Soviet Union, for example, made extensive immigration from Russia possible for the first time in seventy years. In 1991 Russian immigrants outnumbered those from any other country. Great Britain's treaty-lease of Hong Kong will end in 1997, and the Crown Colony will revert to Communist China control. Without doubt immigration from Hong Kong will increase before the China takeover.

Getting the bigotry out of U.S. immigration law took forty years, and our country must make sure that immigration quotas based on race, religion, and ethnic background never return. The present preference criteria for immigrants—family reunification, professional skills needed in the United States, and refugee status—can be and should be looked at closely from time to time. At present those who ponder immigration questions most seriously seem satisfied with the criteria preferences as they are, although some feel that the annual limit of fifty thousand on immigrants with special work skills should be raised. The family reunification preference has support not only for its humanitarian quality but also because immigrants with relatives already in the country are likely to receive some family support upon arrival.

Present law defines refugees as persons who have fled from their country to avoid persecution because of their religious or political beliefs. The plight of Haitians turned back after fleeing hunger and economic chaos in their country has made some people feel that the criteria for refugee status should be changed. The problem—a huge problem —is that refugee status based on wretched poverty would qualify hundreds of millions of people around the world to seek asylum as refugees. The current definition of a refugee seems unlikely to change. Problems such as the Haitians present must concern us deeply because they are on our very doorstep. We should help in every way we can; we should use our influence with the United Nations and the Organization of American States to get those international bodies to help.

A question that Congress will wrestle with often is what the annual total of immigrants should be. Should Congress listen to immigration proponents who argue that immigration is really low, fewer than four immigrants admitted annually for every thousand of the U.S. population? Should they listen to those who say that immigration should be reduced at least for the next ten or twenty years? This reduction, some immigration experts say, would make easier the assimilation of millions of immigrants who arrived during the 1980s. These experts point out that the massive immigration of the first three decades of this century was followed by very limited immigration during the 1930s and 1940s, giving the country time to "digest" the new Americans of that period.

One thing is certain: as far into the future as we can see, many immigrants will continue to come to the United States. They will create problems for some cities and states, problems the federal government should help relieve. But they will continue to bring energy, talent, and cultural richness to America.

Bibliography

Arocha, Zita. "1980s Expected to Set Mark as Top Immigration Decade." *The Washington Post*, July 23, 1988.

Ashabranner, Brent. *An Ancient Heritage: The Arab-American Minority*. New York: HarperCollins Publishers, 1991.

————. *The New Americans: Changing Patterns in U.S. Immigration*. New York: Dodd, Mead & Co., 1983.

————. *The Vanishing Border: A Photographic Journey Along Our Frontier with Mexico*. New York: Dodd, Mead & Co., 1987. (Now distributed by G. P. Putnam's Sons).

———— and Melissa Ashabranner. *Into a Strange Land: Unaccompanied Refugee Youth in America*. New York: Dodd, Mead & Co., 1987. (Reissued by G. P. Putnam's Sons, 1989).

Ashabranner, Melissa and Brent Ashabranner. *Counting America: The Story of the United States Census*. New York: G. P. Putnam's Sons, 1989.

Barone, Michael. "Immigration—Has Our Melting Pot Boiled Over?" *The Washington Post*, October 18, 1987.

Bell, David A. "The Triumph of Asian Americans." *The New Republic*, July 15 and 22, 1985.

Bouvier, Leon F. and Robert W. Gardner. "Immigration to the U.S.: The Unfinished Story." *Population Bulletin*, Vol. 41, No. 4, November 1986. (Population Reference Bureau, Washington, D.C.).

Fainhaus, David. *Lithuanians in the USA: Aspects of Ethnic Identity*. Chicago: Lithuanian Library Press, Inc., 1991. (Translated by Algirdas Dumcius.)

Fischman, Joshua. "A Journey of Hearts and Minds." *Psychology Today*, July 1986.

Fuchs, Lawrence H. *The American Kaleidoscope: Race, Ethnicity, and the Civic Culture*. Hanover, N. H., and London: University Press of New England (Wesleyan University Press), 1990.

Gardner, Robert W., Bryant Robey, and Peter C. Smith. "Asian Americans: Growth, Change, and Diversity." *Population Bulletin*, Vol. 40, No. 4, October 1985. (Population Reference Bureau, Washington, D. C.).

Glazer, Nathan and Daniel P. Moynihan. *Beyond the Melting Pot* (Second edition). Cambridge, Mass.: M.I.T. Press, 1970.

Hanif, Mohammed. "Living the Dream in America." *Washington Business* (*The Washington Post*), October 14, 1991.

Henry, William A. "Beyond the Melting Pot." *Time*, April 9, 1990.

Kennedy, John F. *A Nation of Immigrants*. New York: Anti-defamation League of B'nai B'rith, 1959. (Reissued by Harper and Row, 1986).

Lemieux, Josh. "A Taste of Success." *Columbia Missourian*, March 30, 1988.

Mandel, Michael J. and Christopher Farrell, et al. "The Immigrants: How They're Helping to Revitalize the U.S. Economy." *BusinessWeek*. July 13, 1992.

Marcus, Erin. "More Immigrant Children Face Double Disadvantage." *The Washington Post*, May 24, 1992.

McClester, Cedric. *Kwanzaa*. New York: Gumbs & Thomas, Publishers, 1990.

McCombs, Phil. "Washington's Missionary of Health." *The Washington Post*, June 23, 1992.

Montague, Ashley. *The American Way of Life*. New York: G. P. Putnam's Sons, 1967.

Porter, A. P. *Kwanzaa*. Minneapolis: Carolrhoda Books, Inc., 1991.

Reinhold, Robert. "Flow of Third World Immigrants Alters Weave of U.S. Society." *The New York Times*, June 30, 1986.

Ringle, Ken. "Portal to a Nation of Hope and Fears." *The Washington Post*, September 7, 1990.

Schlesinger, Arthur M., Jr. *The Disuniting of America*. Knoxville, Tenn.: Whittle Direct Books (The Larger Agenda Series), 1991.

Simon, Julian L. *The Economic Consequences of Immigration*. Cambridge, Mass.: Basil Blackwell, Inc., 1989. (Published in association with the Cato Institute).

Turan, Kenneth. "Through the Doors of Ellis Island." *The Washington Post*, December 30, 1990.

Index